"Congratulations, Lia," he said, his voice chilling her. "You've won the jackpot after all. You're about to become a Scott."

"This is not how I wanted this to happen," she said on a throat-aching whisper. Tears pressed the backs of her eyes. She couldn't let them fall.

"You came here," Zach said, his voice hard. "What did you expect? Did you think I would be happy?"

She dropped her gaze. A single tear spilled free and she dashed it away, determined not to cry in front of him. Not to be weak.

"I had hoped you might be, yes." She lifted her chin and sucked back her tears. "Clearly I was mistaken."

"We'll marry," he said. "Because we must. But it's an arrangement, do you understand? We'll do it for as long as necessary, to protect our families, and then we'll end it when the time comes."

SICILY'S CORRETTI DYNASTY

The more powerful the family...the darker the secrets!

Mills & Boon® Modern™ Romance introduces the Correttis:

Sicily's most scandalous family!

Behind the closed doors of their opulent *palazzo*, ruthless desire and the lethal Corretti charm are alive and well.

We invite you to step over the threshold
and enter the Correttis' dark and dazzling world...

The Empire
Young, rich, and notoriously handsome, the Correttis'
legendary exploits regularly feature in Sicily's tabloid pages!

The Scandal
But how long can their reputations withstand the glaring heat
of the spotlight before their family's secrets are exposed?

The Legacy
Once nearly destroyed by the secrets cloaking their thirst
for power, the new generation of Correttis are riding high
again—and no disgrace or scandal will stand in their way...

Sicily's Corretti Dynasty

A LEGACY OF SECRETS
Carol Marinelli

AN INVITATION TO SIN
Sarah Morgan

A SHADOW OF GUILT
Abby Green

AN INHERITANCE OF SHAME
Kate Hewitt

A WHISPER OF DISGRACE
Sharon Kendrick

A FAÇADE TO SHATTER
Lynn Raye Harris

A SCANDAL IN THE HEADLINES
Caitlin Crews

A HUNGER FOR THE FORBIDDEN
Maisey Yates

8 volumes to collect—you won't want to miss out!

A FAÇADE
TO SHATTER

BY
LYNN RAYE HARRIS

First published in Great Britain 2013
by Mills & Boon, an imprint of Harlequin (UK) Limited.
Harlequin (UK) Limited, Eton House, 18-24 Paradise Road,
Richmond, Surrey TW9 1SR

© Harlequin Books S.A. 2013

Special thanks and acknowledgement are given to Lynn Raye Harris for her contribution to *Sicily's Corretti Dynasty* series

ISBN: 978 0 263 23560 9

Harlequin (UK) policy is to use papers that are natural, renewable and recyclable products and made from wood grown in sustainable forests. The logging and manufacturing process conform to the legal environmental regulations of the country of origin.

Printed and bound in Great Britain
by CPI Antony Rowe, Chippenham, Wiltshire

Lynn Raye Harris read her first Mills & Boon® romance when her grandmother carted home a box from a yard sale. She didn't know she wanted to be a writer then, but she definitely knew she wanted to marry a sheikh or a prince and live the glamorous life she read about in the pages. Instead she married a military man and moved around the world. These days she makes her home in North Alabama, with her handsome husband and two crazy cats. Writing for Harlequin Mills & Boon® is a dream come true. You can visit her at www.lynnrayeharris.com

Recent titles by the same author:

A GAME WITH ONE WINNER
REVELATIONS OF THE NIGHT BEFORE
UNNOTICED AND UNTOUCHED
MARRIAGE BEHIND THE FAÇADE

**Did you know these are also available as eBooks?
Visit www.millsandboon.co.uk**

For all those who serve in the armed forces,
thank you for your service.

CHAPTER ONE

ZACH SCOTT DIDN'T do parties. Not anymore.

Once, he'd been the life of the party. But everything had changed a little over a year ago. Zach shoved his hands into his tuxedo trouser pockets and frowned. He'd thought coming to Sicily with a friend, in order to attend a wedding, would be an easy thing to do. There'd been no wedding, it had turned out, but the reception was taking place anyway. And he stood on the edge of the ballroom, wondering where Taylor Carmichael had got to. Wondering if he could slip away and text his regrets to her.

His head was pounding after a rough night. He'd been dreaming again. Dreaming of guns and explosions and planes plummeting from the sky.

There was nothing like a fight for survival to rearrange a man's priorities. Since his plane had been shot down in enemy territory, the kinds of things he'd once done—fundraisers, public appearances, speeches, political dinners—were now a kind of torture he'd prefer to live without.

Except it was more impossible to get out of those things now than ever before. Not only was he Zachariah James Scott IV, son of an eminent United States senator and heir to a pharmaceuticals fortune, he was also a returning military hero.

Zach's frown deepened.

Since his rescue—in which every single marine sent to extract him had perished—he'd been in demand as a sort of all-American poster boy. The media couldn't get enough of him, and he knew a big part of that was his father's continual use of his story in his public appearances.

Zachariah J. Scott III wasn't about to let the story die. Not when it could do him a world of political good.

His son had done his duty when he could have chosen an easier path. *His* son had chosen to serve his country instead of himself. It was true that Zach could have sat on the Scott Pharmaceuticals board and moved mountains of money instead of flying jets into a war zone. But the jets were a part of him.

Or had been a part of him until the crash had left him with crushing, unpredictable headaches that made it too dangerous to fly.

Yes, everyone loved that he'd bravely gone to war and survived.

Except he didn't feel brave, and he damn sure didn't feel like he'd done anything extraordinary. He didn't want the attention, didn't deserve the accolades. He'd failed pretty spectacularly, in his opinion.

But he couldn't make them stop. So he stood stiffly and smiled for the cameras like a dutiful military man should, and he felt dead inside. And the deader he felt, the more interested the media seemed to get.

It wasn't all bad, though. He'd taken over the stewardship of the Scott Foundation, his family's charitable arm, and he worked tirelessly to promote military veterans' causes. They often came back with so little, and with their lives shattered. The government tried to take care of them, but it was a huge job—and sometimes they fell through the cracks.

It was Zach's goal to save as many of them as he could. He owed it to them, by God.

He made a visual sweep of the room. At least the media attention wasn't directed at him right now. The Sicilian media was far more interested in the fact the bride had jilted the groom at the altar. Zach was of no interest whatsoever to this crowd. That, at least, was a bonus.

It wasn't often he could move anonymously through a gathering like this one.

Still, he was on edge, as if he were being followed. He prowled the edges of the crowd in the darkened ballroom, his headache barely under control as he searched for Taylor. She wasn't answering his texts, and he was growing concerned. She'd been so worried about this trip, about her return to acting, and about the director's opinion of her.

But Taylor was tough, and he knew she would have gone into the press event with her head held high. She wanted this film badly, wanted the money and respectability for the veterans' clinic back in Washington, D.C., where she'd spent so much time working to help others. He thought of the soldiers, sailors, airmen and marines—most suffering the debilitating effects of posttraumatic stress—the clinic helped, thought of the constant need for funding, and knew that Taylor would have entered that room determined to succeed.

What he didn't know was how it had turned out.

He stepped into a quiet corner—if there was such a thing—and reached into his breast pocket for his phone. A small medal hanging from a ribbon came out with it, and he blinked as he realized what it was. The Distinguished Flying Cross he'd been awarded after returning from the high Afghan desert. Taylor must have put it in there when she'd picked up the tux from the cleaners for him. He fingered the starburst, squeezed it in his palm before putting it back into his pocket.

He hadn't wanted the medal, but he hadn't had a choice. There were other medals, too, which his father never failed to mention in his speeches, but Zach just wanted to forget them all.

Taylor insisted he had to realize he deserved them. She meant well, damn her, but she drove him crazier than any sister ever could have.

He dialed Taylor's number impatiently. No answer. Frustration hammered into him. He wanted to know she was all right, and he wanted to escape this room. The crowd was swelling—never let it be said that Sicilians let a chance to party go to waste—and the noise level was growing louder.

He was in no mood.

He turned toward the exit just as the DJ blared the first track and the crowd cheered. The lights went completely out and strobe lights flashed. Zach's heart began to thud painfully. Against his will, he shrank into the wall, breathing hard.

It's just a party, just a party. But the flashes didn't stop, people started to shout, and he couldn't fight the panic dragging him down any longer.

No, no, no...

Suddenly he was back in the trench, in the pitch of night, the bursts of gunfire and explosives all around him, the thrumming of their bass boom ricocheting into his breastbone, making his body ache with the pressure. He closed his eyes, swallowed hard, his throat full of sand and dust and grit.

Violence and frustration bloomed inside his gut. He wanted to fight, wanted to surge upright and grab a gun, wanted to help the marines hold off the enemy. But they'd drugged him, because he'd broken his leg, and he couldn't move.

He lay helpless, his eyes squeezed tight—and then he felt a soft hand on his arm. The hand moved along his upper arm, ghosted over his cheek. The touch of skin on skin broke his paralysis.

He reacted with the instincts of a warrior, grabbing the hand and twisting it until the owner cried out. The cry was soft, feminine, not at all that of a terrorist bent on destroying him. Vaguely, he realized the body pressed against his was not rough. It was clad in something satiny that slid against the fabric of his own clothing.

He forced his eyes open after long moments. The lights still flashed, and his heart still pumped adrenaline into his body. He blinked and shook his head. Was he not in the desert? Was he not the last one alive in the trench?

The sounds began to separate themselves until he could pick out music, laughter and loud conversation. He focused on the elegant paneled wall in front of him—and realized he held a woman against it, her hand high up behind her back. He could hear her panting softly.

"Please," she said, her voice calmer than he expected it to be. "I don't think I am who you think I am."

Who he thought she was? Zach blinked. Who did he think she was?

A terrorist. Someone bent on killing him.

But she wasn't, was she? He was in Sicily, at the infamous Corretti wedding, and this woman was a guest. Her blue-green eyes were set in a pretty face. Dark hair was piled on top of her head, and her breasts strained against the fabric of her gown, threatening to pop free at any moment. He hadn't spun her around, but instead held her against the wall with his body practically wrapped around hers.

One hand held hers behind her back, nearly between her shoulder blades, while the other gripped her jaw and forced her head back against the paneling. Her soft curves melded against him, filling all the hard angles of his body in ways he hadn't experienced in a very long time.

He'd had no room for softness in his life since returning from the war. He'd viewed it as something of a regret, but a necessary one. Now, he found that he was starving for the contact. His body began to stir, the telltale thrum of blood in his groin taking him by surprise.

Zach let the woman go as if she'd burned him and took a hasty step backward. What the hell was wrong with him? This was why he didn't like public appearances anymore—what if he lost his mind the way he just had? What would the media say then?

Son of a bitch.

"Forgive me," he said tightly.

"Are you all right?" she asked.

It was such a normal question, in response to an abnormal situation, and yet he couldn't formulate an answer. He simply wanted to escape. For once, instead of standing stoically and enduring whatever was flung at him, he wanted out.

There was no one here to stop him, no reporters or cameras, no duty pressing him to remain where he was and endure.

He turned blindly, seeking an exit. Somehow, he found a door and burst through it, into the cool and quiet hallway. Behind him, he heard movement. He didn't know why he turned, but he did.

She was there, watching him. Her hair was dark red and her dress a shocking shade of pink that looked as if it was about to split across her generous breasts.

"Are you all right?" she asked again.

"Fine," he replied in crisp Italian. "I apologize. You startled me."

She came forward then, hesitantly, her hands clasped together in front of her. She was lovely, he decided, in spite of the horrible dress. Her shape was imprinted on his mind, her curves still burning into his body. His hands itched to explore her, but he kept them clenched into fists at his sides. He used to take whatever women offered him, as often as they offered it, but that man had ceased to exist in the months after he'd returned from the war.

At first, he'd indulged in sex because he'd thought it would help him forget. It hadn't. It had only sharpened the contrast between life and death, only made him feel worse instead of better.

Now, denying himself was a matter of routine. Not to mention safer for all involved. His dreams were too unpredictable to sleep with a woman at his side.

Worse, they seemed to be sliding into his waking life if what had just happened was any indication.

The woman was still looking at him. Blue-green eyes fringed in dark lashes blinked up at him as a line formed on her forehead. "You really don't look well."

He glanced down at her hands, at the way she rubbed the thumb of one hand into her wrist. He'd hurt her, and it sickened him. What kind of man had he become? He was coming unglued inside, and no one could help him.

"I'm fine," he clipped out. "I'm sorry I hurt you."

Her eyes dropped. "You didn't really. You just surprised me."

"You're lying," he said, and her head snapped up, her eyes searching his. Something in those eyes called to him, but he shut it off and backed away.

"You don't know that," she replied, her chin lifting. "You don't know me."

He almost believed her. But her lip trembled, ruining her brave façade, and Zach loathed himself. "You should go," he said. "Walk away. It's safer."

She blinked. "Safer? Are you so dangerous, then?"

He swallowed. "Perhaps."

Her gaze was steady. Penetrating. "I'm not afraid," she

said softly. "And I don't think you're dangerous to anyone but yourself."

Her words hit him like a punch to the gut. No one had ever said that to him before. The truth of it was sharper than any blade.

More frightening.

Anger and despair flowed over him in waves. He wanted to be normal again, wanted to be what he'd once been. But he couldn't seem to dig out of the morass, and he hated himself for it. He simply didn't know what normal was anymore.

"I'm sorry," he said again, because there was nothing else he could say. And then he turned and strode away.

Lia Corretti sucked in a disappointed breath as she watched the tall, dark American striding down the hall away from her. Something fell from his hand and bounced on the plush carpet. Lia hurried forward, calling to him.

He did not turn back. She stooped to pick up the small object on the floor. It was some kind of military medal suspended from a red, white and blue ribbon. She clutched it in her hand and looked down the long corridor at his retreating back. He walked so precisely, so stiffly, with the bearing of a soldier.

Of course he did.

She looked at the medal again. He'd dropped it on purpose. She did not doubt that. She'd seen his fingers open, seen the shiny object tumble to the floor, but he hadn't stopped to retrieve it.

Why?

Her wrist still smarted where he'd twisted it behind her back. She didn't think he'd been aware of what he'd been doing. He'd seemed…distant, as if he were somewhere else. It's what had made her go to him, what had made her touch him and ask if he was all right. He'd been plastered against that wall, his eyes squeezed tight shut, and she'd thought he'd been ill.

Lia closed her fingers around the medal. It was warm from his skin, and her heart skipped. She could still see the raw look on his face when he'd realized what he was doing to her.

She knew that look. It was one of self-loathing, one of relief and one of confusion all rolled into one. She knew it because she'd lived with those feelings her entire life.

In that moment, she'd felt a kinship with him. It was so strange. After a lifetime of isolation, one moment of looking into a stranger's eyes had made her feel less alone than she'd ever felt before.

She turned to go back into the ballroom, though she'd rather be anywhere else, and caught a glimpse of her reflection in one of the full-length mirrors lining the corridor. Revulsion shuddered through her.

No wonder he'd wanted to get away.

She was a whale. A giant pink whale bursting at the seams. She'd been so excited when she'd been asked to be a bridesmaid. She'd finally thought she might be accepted by the sleek, beautiful Corretti family, but instead she'd been forced into a blazing pink dress at least two sizes too small for her bust. Carmela Corretti had laughed when she'd walked out of the fitting room, but she'd promised to have the dress fixed.

She hadn't, of course.

Lia's grandmother was the only one who'd seemed to sympathize. When Lia put the dress on today, despair and humiliation rolling through her in giant waves, her grandmother had hugged her tight and told her she was beautiful.

Tears pricked Lia's eyes. Teresa Corretti was the only one in the family who had ever been kind to her. Her grandfather hadn't been unkind, precisely, but he'd always frightened her. She still couldn't believe he was gone. He'd loomed so large in her life that she'd started to think him immortal. He'd been intense, driven, the kind of man no one crossed. But now he was dead, and the family wasn't any closer than they'd ever been. Not only that, but Lia wasn't certain that her cousin Alessandro wasn't to be more feared as the new head of the family.

Lia screwed up her courage and reentered the ballroom. A glance at her watch told her she'd put in enough time to call it an evening. She was going to find her grandmother and tell her she was leaving. No one would care that she was gone anyway.

The music pumped and thumped as it had before, and the crowd surged. But then another sound lifted over the din. It took Lia a minute to realize it was Carmela, shrieking drunkenly.

Lia despised her late uncle's wife, but thankfully she hardly ever had to be around the woman. She didn't care what Carmela's problem was tonight. She just wanted to go back to her room and get out of this awful dress. She'd curl up with a book or something inane on television and try to forget the humiliations of the day.

But, before she could find her grandmother, the music suddenly died and the crowd parted as if Moses himself were standing there.

Everyone turned to look at Lia. She shrank instinctively under the scrutiny, her heart pounding. Was this yet another ploy of Carmela's to embarrass her? Did she really have to endure another scene? What had she ever done to the woman?

But it wasn't Carmela who caught her attention. It was Rosa. Carmela's daughter stood there, her face pale, her eyes fixed on her mother's face.

"That's right," Carmela said gleefully, her voice rising over the sudden silence of the gathered crowd, "Benito Corretti is your father, not Carlo! That one is your sister," she

spat, pointing a red-tipped finger at Lia as if she were a particularly loathsome bug. "Be thankful you did not turn out
like her. She's useless—fat and mousy and weak!"

Rosa looked stricken. Lia's heart stuttered in her chest.
She had a sister? She wasn't close with her three half-brothers. She wasn't close with anyone. But a sister?

She'd never had anyone, not really. She'd often longed
for a sister, someone she might get to know in a way she
couldn't get to know brothers. Her three half-brothers had
one another. Plus they were men. A sister, however—that
felt different somehow.

A surge of hope flooded her then. Perhaps she wasn't really alone in this family, after all. She had a sister.

A sister who was every bit as lost at this moment as Lia
had been her entire life. She could see it on Rosa's face, and
she wanted to help. It was the one thing she had to offer that
she knew was valuable. But suddenly, Rosa was storming
away from Carmela, coming across the room straight for Lia.
She reached out instinctively to comfort her when she came
near. But Rosa didn't stop. The look she gave Lia could have
frozen lava. Lia's heart cracked as Rosa shoved her hands
away with a growled, "Don't!"

A throb of pain ricocheted through her chest where her
heart had been. Rejection was nothing new to her, but the
freshness of it in the face of her hope was almost too much.
She stood there for long moments after Rosa had gone, aware
of the eyes upon her.

Aware of the pity.

Soon, before she could think of a single pithy remark,
the crowd turned away, their attention waning. Self-loathing
flooded her. No wonder Rosa hadn't wanted her comfort. She
was so pitiful. So naive.

How many times had she let her heart open? How many

times had she had the door slammed in her face? When was she going to learn to guard herself better?

Shame and anger coiled together inside her belly. Why couldn't she be decisive? Brave? Why did she care how they treated her?

Why couldn't she just tell them all to go to hell the way her mother would have done?

Grace Hart had been beautiful, perfect, a gorgeous movie star who'd been swept off her feet by Benito Corretti. She'd had no problem handling the Correttis, until she'd accidentally driven her car off a cliff and left Benito a lonely widower with a baby. Soon after that, Benito had sent Lia to live with Salvatore and Teresa.

She knew why he'd done it. Because she wasn't beautiful and perfect like her mother. Because she was shy and awkward and lacking in the most basic graces. She'd grown up on the periphery, watching her cousins and half-siblings from a distance. Wanting her father's love but getting only cool silence.

No, she wasn't beautiful and perfect, and she wasn't decisive. She hated crowds, and she hated pretending she fit in when everyone knew she didn't. She was a failure.

She wanted to go home, back to her small cottage at Salvatore and Teresa's country estate, back to her books and her garden. She loved getting her fingers in the dirt, loved creating something beautiful from nothing more than soil and water and seeds. It gave her hope somehow that she wasn't as inconsequential as she always felt.

Useless. Fat and mousy and weak.

Lia turned and fled through the same door Rosa had stormed out of. This was it. The final straw in her long, tortured life as a Corretti. She was finished pretending to fit in.

She meant to go to her room, but instead she marched out

through the courtyard and found herself standing in front of the swimming pool.

There was no one in it tonight. The hotel had been over-run with wedding guests, and they were all at the reception. The air was hot, and the blue water was so clear, the pool lit from below with soft lights. For a moment Lia thought of jumping in with her dress on. It would ruin the stupid thing, but she hardly cared.

She stood there for a long time, hot feelings swelling within her. She wanted to be decisive. Brave. She wanted to make her own decisions, and she didn't want to let anyone make her feel inferior or unneeded ever again.

She took a step closer to the edge of the pool, staring down into the depths of the water. It would ruin her dress, her shoes, her hair.

So what?

For the first time in a long time, she was going to do what she wanted. She was going to step into the pool and ruin her dress, and she damn well didn't care. She was going to wash away the pain of the day and emerge clean. A new, determined Lia.

Before she could change her mind, she kicked off her shoes and stepped over the edge, letting the water take her down. It closed over her head so peacefully, shutting out all the sounds from above. Shutting out the pain and anger, the humiliation of this day.

She didn't fight it, didn't kick or struggle. She was a strong swimmer, and she wasn't afraid. She just let the water take her down to the bottom, where everything was still. She'd only sit here a moment, and then she'd kick to the top again.

Above her, she heard some kind of noise. And then the water rippled as someone leaped into the pool with her. It annoyed her. She wasn't finished being quiet and still.

Guests from the reception, no doubt. Drunk and looking for a good time.

Lia started to kick upward again, her solace interrupted now. She would get out of the pool and drag her sodden body back to her room. But her dress was heavier than she'd thought, twisting around her legs and pulling her back down again.

She kicked harder, but got nowhere. And then she realized with a sinking feeling that the suction of the drain had trapped part of her skirt. Panic bloomed inside her as she kicked harder.

Stupid, stupid, stupid.

She couldn't cry for help, couldn't do anything but try to rip herself out of the pink mess.

The dress didn't want to come off. Her lungs ached. Any minute and they would burst.

She kicked harder—but she was caught by her own folly.

No, by Carmela's folly, she thought numbly. Carmela's folly of a dress. Wouldn't everyone laugh when they discovered her bloated body in the pool tomorrow?

Poor, pitiful, stupid Lia. She'd been decisive, all right. She'd made a decision that was going to kill her. She wondered if her mother had thought the same thing in those seconds when her car had hung suspended over the cliffs before plunging onto the rocks below....

CHAPTER TWO

LIA WOKE SLOWLY. She coughed, her throat and chest aching as she did so. She remembered being in the pool, remembered her dress getting caught. She pushed herself up on an elbow. She was in a darkened room. She sat upright, and the sheet slid down her body. How had she gotten out of the pool? And why was she naked? She didn't remember going back to her room, didn't remember anything but that last moment where she'd thought of the Correttis finding her pink-clad body trapped at the bottom of the pool.

She pushed the sheet back, intending to get out of the bed, but a movement in the darkness arrested her.

"I wouldn't do that if I were you," a deep male voice said.

Lia grabbed the sheet and yanked it back up. How long had he been standing there?

"Who are you? And why are you in my room?"

His laugh was dry. "I'm Zach. And you're in my room, sugar."

Sugar. "You're American," she said, her heart thumping steadily. The same American as earlier?

"I'm sorry," he said.

"For what?"

"You sound disappointed."

She shook her head, stopping when her brain couldn't quite keep up. She felt light-headed, as if she'd been drinking, when she hadn't had more than a single glass of champagne all evening.

"How did I get here?"

"I carried you."

"Impossible," she scoffed. She was tall and awkward and fat. He couldn't have done it without a cart and a team of horses to pull her.

"Clearly not," he told her. "Because you're here."

"But why?" The last thing she remembered was water and darkness.

Wait, that wasn't right. There'd also been light, a hard surface under her back and the scalding taste of chlorine in her throat.

"Because you begged me not to call anyone when I pulled you out of the pool."

She vaguely recalled it. She remembered that she'd been worried about anyone seeing her, about them laughing and pointing. About Carmela standing there, slim arms folded, evil face twisted in a smirk, nodding and laughing…fat and mousy and weak.

"It was the only thing you said. Repeatedly," he added, and Lia wanted to hide.

She put a hand to her head. Her hair was still damp, though not soaked. And she was naked. Utterly, completely naked. Her face flamed.

He sat beside her on the bed, holding out a glass of water. "Here, take this," he said, his voice gentle.

She looked up, met his gaze—and her heart skipped several beats in a row. It was the same man. He had dark eyes, a hard jaw and the beginnings of a scruff where he hadn't shaved in hours. His hair was cropped short, almost military style, and his lips were just about the sexiest thing she'd ever seen in her life.

She took the water and drank deeply, choking when she'd

had too much. He grabbed the glass and set it aside, no doubt ready to pound her on the back if she needed it. She held a hand up, stopping him before he could do so.

"I'm fine," she squeaked out. "Thank you."

He sat back and watched her carefully. "Are you certain?"

She looked at him again—and realized his expression was full of pity. Pity! It was almost more than she could bear to have one more person look at her like that tonight.

"Yes."

"You were lucky tonight," he said, his voice hardening. "Next time, there might not be anyone to pull you out."

She knew he was trying to say something important, but she was too weary to figure out what it was. And then his meaning hit her.

"I wasn't trying to kill myself," she protested. "It was an accident."

He raised an eyebrow. "I saw you step into the water. You just decided to go swimming while fully dressed?"

She dropped her gaze from his. "Something like that." What would he know of it if she told him the real reason? He was beautiful, perfect. She'd thought they had something in common earlier tonight, but she'd been wrong.

Of course.

She usually was. It disappointed her more than she could say. And made her feel lonelier than ever. This man, whatever his flaws, had nothing in common with her. How could he?

"What's your name?" he asked, his voice turning soft.

"Lia. And I hated my dress, if you must know. That's why I jumped in the pool."

His bark of laughter surprised her. "Then why did you buy it in the first place?"

"I didn't. It was a bridesmaid dress, and it was hideous."

"Pink is not your color, I'm sorry to say." His voice was too warm to take offense. "Definitely not." She was slightly confused, given his reaction to her earlier, and more than a little curious about him. It occurred to her she should be apprehensive to be alone with a strange man, in his room, while she was naked beneath his sheets.

But she wasn't. Paradoxically, he made her feel safe. As if he would stand between her and the world if she asked him to. It wasn't true, of course, but it was a nice feeling for the moment.

"I'm afraid I couldn't save the dress," he said. "It tore in the drain, and the rest rather disintegrated once I tried to remove it."

She felt heat creeping into her cheeks again. "You removed everything, I see."

"Yes, sorry, but I didn't want you soaking my sheets. Or getting sick from lying around in cold, clammy clothing."

What did she say to that? *Did you like what you saw? Thank you? I hope you weren't terribly inconvenienced?*

Lia cleared her throat and hoped she didn't look as embarrassed as she felt. "Did you find your medal?"

It was the most benign thing she could think of. She'd tucked it into her cleavage when she'd returned to the ballroom. She would regret it if it were lost. Something about it had seemed important to her, even if he'd cast it aside so easily.

"I did."

"Why did you drop it?" It seemed a harmless topic. Far safer than the subject of her body, no doubt.

"I have my reasons," he said coolly.

Lia waited, but he didn't say anything else. "If you intend to throw it away again, I'll keep it." She didn't know where that had come from, but she meant it. It seemed wrong to throw something like that away.

"It's yours if you want it," he said after a taut moment in

which she thought she saw regret and anger scud across his handsome face.

She sensed there were currents swirling beneath the surface that she just didn't understand. But she wanted to. "What did you get it for?"

He shoved a hand through his hair. She watched the muscles bunch in his forearm, swallowed. He'd been in a tuxedo the last time she'd seen him, but now he wore a dark T-shirt that clung to the well-defined muscles of his chest and arms, and a pair of faded jeans. His feet, she noted, were bare.

So sexy.

"Flying," he said.

"Flying? You are a pilot?"

"I was."

"What happened?" His face clouded, and she realized she'd gone too far. She wanted to know why he'd reacted the way he had in the ballroom, but she could tell she'd crossed a line with her question. Whatever it was caused him pain, and it was not her right to know anything more than she already did.

"Never mind. Don't answer that," she told him before he could speak.

He shrugged, as if it were nothing. She sensed it was everything. "It's no secret. I went to war. I got shot down. My flying days are over."

He said it with such finality, such bittersweet grace, that it made her ache for him. "I'm sorry."

"Why?" His dark eyes gleamed as he watched her.

"Because you seem sad about it," she said truthfully. And haunted, if his reaction in the ballroom earlier was any indication. What could happen to make a man react that way? She didn't understand it, but she imagined he'd been through something terrible. And that made her hurt for him.

He sighed. "I wish I could still fly, yes. But we don't always get to do what we want, do we?"

Lia shook her head. "Definitely not."

He leaned forward until she could smell him—warm spice, a hint of chlorine. "What's your story, Lia?"

She licked her lips. "Story?"

"Why are you here? What do you regret?"

She didn't want to tell him she was a Corretti. Not yet. If he were here at the wedding, he was someone's guest. She just didn't know whose guest he was. And she didn't want to know. Somehow, it would spoil everything.

"I was a bridesmaid," she said, shrugging.

"And what do you regret?" His dark eyes were intent on hers, and she felt as if her blood had turned to hot syrup in her veins.

"I regret that I agreed to wear that dress," she said, trying to lighten the mood.

He laughed in response, and answering warmth rolled through her. "You'll never have to wear it again, I assure you."

"Then I owe you an even bigger debt of gratitude than I thought."

His gaze dropped, lingered on her mouth. Her breath shortened as if he'd caressed her lips with a finger instead of with his eyes. She found herself wishing he would kiss her more than she'd ever wished for anything.

He sat there for a long minute, his body leaning toward hers even as she leaned toward him. Her heart thrummed as the distance between them closed inch by tiny inch.

Suddenly, he swore and shot up from the bed. A light switched on, and she realized he'd gone to the desk nearby. The light was low, but it still made her blink against the sudden intrusion into her retinas.

"You don't owe me anything." His voice was rough, and it scraped over her nerve endings. Made her shiver.

She blinked up at him. He stood there with his hands shoved in his pockets, watching her. A lock of hair fell across her face, and she pushed it back, tucking it behind her ear.

Zach's gaze sharpened. He watched her with such an intense expression on his face. But she couldn't decide what he was feeling. Desire? Irritation? Disdain?

Dio, she was naive. She hated it. She imagined Rosa would have known what to do with this man. Lia wished she could talk to her sister, ask her advice—but how silly was that? Rosa was as estranged from her as she'd ever been. This new connection between them meant nothing to Rosa.

Lia's hair fell across her face again and she combed her fingers through it, wincing at how tangled it was. She would need a lot of conditioner to get this mess sorted.

She looked up at Zach, and her heart stopped beating. His expression was stark, focused—and she realized that the sheet had slipped down to reveal the curve of a breast. Her first instinct was to yank the fabric up again.

But she didn't.

She couldn't.

The air seemed to grow thicker between them. He didn't move or speak. Neither did she. It was as if time sat still, waiting for them.

"Are you staying in the hotel?" Zach asked abruptly, and the bubble of yearning pulsing between them seemed to pop.

Lia closed her eyes and tried to slow her reckless heart. "I am," she told him.

What did she know of desire, other than what she'd read in romance novels? Her experience of men was limited to a few awkward dates to please her grandmother. She'd been kissed—groped on one memorable occasion—but that was the sum total of her sexual experience. Whatever had been going on here, she was certain she had it wrong. Zach did not want her.

Which he proved in the next few seconds. He turned away and pulled open a drawer. Then he threw something at her.

"Get dressed. I'll take you back to your room."

Embarrassment warred with anger as her fingers curled into the fabric of a white T-shirt. "This will hardly do the job," she said, turning to self-deprecation when what she really wanted to do was run back to her room and hide beneath the covers. *Fat and mousy and weak.*

"Put it on and I'll get a robe from the closet."

Lia snorted in spite of herself. "The walk of shame without the shame. How droll."

He moved closer, his gaze sharpening again, and her heart pounded. "And is that what you want, Lia? Shame?"

Between the horrendous dress she'd had to wear while people stared and pointed, to the very public brush-off she'd had from Rosa, she'd had enough shame today to last her for a while.

Lia shrugged lightly, though inside she felt anything but light. She was wound tight, ready to scream, but she wouldn't. Not until she was back in her room and could bury her face in the pillow first.

"A figure of speech," she said. "Now turn around if you want me to put this on."

He hesitated for a long moment. But then he did as she said, and she dropped the sheet and tugged the shirt into place. It was bigger than she'd thought, but she still had her doubts it would cover her bottom when she stood. She scooted to the edge of the bed and put her legs over the side.

She stood gingerly. Her head swam a little, but she was mostly fine. The shirt barely covered her bottom, but it managed.

"I'll take that robe now," she said imperiously.

Zach walked over to the closet and pulled out a white, fluffy Corretti Hotel robe. Then he turned and brought it back to her, his gaze unreadable as he handed it over. He did a good job of keeping his eyes locked on hers—

But then they dropped, skimming over her breasts—which tingled in response, the nipples tightening beneath his gaze— then farther down to the tops of her naked thighs, before snapping back to her face. His eyes glittered darkly, and a sharp feeling knifed into her.

If she were a brave woman, a more experienced woman, she'd close the distance between them and put her arms around his neck.

But she wasn't, and she didn't. She was just a silly virgin standing here in a man's T-shirt and wishing he would take her in his arms and kiss her.

Lia shrugged into the robe and tied it tight around her waist. "Thank you for your help, but there's no need for you to come with me. I can find my own way back to my room."

"I insist," he said, taking her elbow in a light but firm grip.

She pulled away. "And I'd rather you didn't."

"It's nonnegotiable, sugar."

Something snapped inside her then. Lia lifted her chin. She was so very tired of people telling her what to do. Of not being taken seriously or respected in any way. She was tired enough of it that she was done putting up with it.

This day, as they say, had been the last straw.

Lia plopped down on the edge of the bed and performed her first overt act of defiance as she crossed one leg over the other and said, "I suppose I'm staying here, then."

Zach fought the urge to grind his teeth. It was everything he could do not to push her back on the bed and untie that robe. His body was painfully hard. Lia tossed her hair again—that hot, tangled mess that was somehow sexier than any polished style could have been—and Zach suppressed the groan that wanted to climb up his throat.

Nothing about this woman was typical. She wasn't afraid of him, she didn't seem to want to impress him and she'd jumped into a pool fully clothed because she hated her dress. And now she sat there glaring at him because he was trying to be a gentleman—for once in his life—and make sure she got back to her room safely.

She crossed her arms beneath her breasts and he fought the urge to go to her, to tunnel his fingers into the thick mass of her auburn hair and lift her mouth to his.

That was what she needed, damn it—a hot, thorough, commanding kiss.

Hell, she needed more than that, but he wasn't going to do any of it. No matter that she seemed to want him to.

And why not?

Tonight, he was a man who'd dragged a drowning woman from a pool, a man who hadn't had sex in so long he'd nearly forgotten what it was like. He wasn't a senator's son or an all-American hero. He wasn't a broken and battered war vet. He was just a man who was interested in a woman for the first time in a long time.

More than interested. His body had been hard from the moment he'd stripped her out of that sodden pink dress, her creamy golden skin and dusky pink nipples firing his blood. He'd tried not to look, tried to view the task with ruthless efficiency, but her body was so lush and beautiful that it would take a man made of stone not to react.

Holy hell.

She stared at him defiantly, her chin lifting, and he had an overwhelming urge to master her. To push her back on the bed, peel open that robe and take what he wanted. Would she be as hot as those smoldering eyes seemed to say she would? Would she burn him to a crisp if he dared to give in to this urgent need?

"If you stay, you might get more than you bargained for," he growled. Because he was primed, on edge, ready to explode. It had been so long since he'd felt desire that to feel it now was a huge adrenaline rush.

Like flying.

"I've already had more than I bargained for today," she said hotly, color flooding her cheeks. "I've had to parade around in front of everyone in a hideous dress that made me look even fatter than I am. I've had to endure the whispers and stares, the laughter, the humiliation."

Zach blinked. Fat? No way. But of course she would think so. Women always did, unless they happened to be about five-six and weighed one hundred pounds. This one was taller than that, about five eight or so, and stacked with curves. She wasn't willowy. And she damn sure wasn't fat.

She choked out a laugh. "I also found out I have a sister—of course, she wants nothing to do with me—and on top of all of that, I finally did something daring and jumped in the pool fully clothed, only to nearly drown."

She sucked in a sharp breath, and he knew she was hovering on the edge of tears. "And then I wake up here, with you, completely naked—"

He thought she was going to cry, but she got to her feet suddenly, her eyes blazing, her chin thrusting in the air, though he could see that it still trembled. Her hands were fists at her sides.

"Even then, the only reaction I arouse in you is pity. I'm naked in front of a man and all he thinks about is the quickest way to get rid of me—so you will excuse me if I fail to cower before this latest pronouncement!"

Zach could only stare at her, mesmerized. He'd have sworn she was going to cry, sworn she would blubber and fall apart—but she hadn't. She was staring at him now, two high red spots on her cheeks, her dark auburn hair tumbling over her shoulders, her eyes flashing fire. The robe had slipped open a bit, exposing the inside of a creamy thigh.

Lust flooded him until he had to react or explode. He meant to turn away, meant to put distance between them. Hell, he meant to walk out of the room and not come back—

But instead, he closed the distance between them, gripped her shoulders as he bent toward her.

"Pity is the last thing I feel for you, Lia," he grated, still determined in some part of his brain to push her away before it was too late.

But then he tugged her closer, until she pressed against him, until she'd have to be stupid not to know what he was thinking about right now.

She gasped, and a skein of hot need uncoiled within him.

"Does this feel like pity?" he growled, his hands sliding down to grip her hips and pull her fully into him.

Her eyes grew large in her lovely face, liquid. For the barest of moments, he thought she seemed too innocent, too sweet. But then she reached up and put a palm to his cheek. Her thumb ghosted over his lips. He couldn't suppress a shudder of longing.

"No," she said, her voice barely more than a whisper. "It doesn't."

He thought there was a note of wonder in her voice, but he ignored it and pressed on, sliding a hand around to cup her round bottom. She wasn't fat, the stupid woman. She was curvaceous, with generously proportioned boobs and hips that other women could only envy.

"Is this what you want, Lia?" he asked, dipping his head, sliding his lips along her cheek in surrender to the hot feelings pounding through him.

Her only answer was a soft gasp. Desire scorched into

him, hammered in his veins. He'd wanted her to go back to her room, wanted to remove the temptation when he had no idea what might happen if he had sex with her, but now that she was in his arms, sending her away had suddenly become impossible.

Her arms went around his neck, and he shuddered. She should be frightened of him after what had happened in the ballroom, but she showed no fear whatsoever. Then again, he had been the one to pull her from the water. Perhaps that redeemed him somewhat in her eyes.

"Why aren't you afraid of me?" he asked against the soft skin of her throat.

"I'm only afraid you'll stop," she said, and he squeezed her to him in reaction as emotions overwhelmed him.

He wanted to tell her not to trust him, wanted to tell her to run far and fast, that he could give her nothing more than a night of passion. He wanted to, but he couldn't find the voice right now. Not when what he so desperately wanted to do was slide his tongue into her mouth and see if she tasted as sweet as she looked.

Zach drew back just enough to see her face. Her eyes were closed, dark lashes fanning her cheekbones, and her pink lips parted on a sigh. She arched her body into his and heat streaked through him. It had been so long. Too long…

He shouldn't do this. He really shouldn't. He didn't know this woman at all.

But it felt like he did. Like he'd known her for ages.

With a groan, Zach fell headlong into temptation.

CHAPTER THREE

As ZACH'S MOUTH came down on hers, Lia's first thought was
to freeze. Her second was to melt into his kiss. She'd been
kissed before, but nothing like this. Nothing with this kind
of heat or raw passion. He wanted her. He *really* wanted her.
This was not a dream, or a fever, or an illusion. This was a
man—a hot, mysterious, dangerous man—and he wanted
her, Lia Corretti.

His tongue slid against hers, and she shivered with longing. She didn't really know what she was doing—but she
knew how it was supposed to feel, how she was supposed
to react.

And she had no problem reacting. Lia arched into him,
met his tongue eagerly, if somewhat inexpertly. She just
hoped he didn't realize it.

The kiss was hot, thrilling, stomach-churning in a good
way. Her body ached with the sudden need to feel more than
this. To feel everything.

She knew she shouldn't be doing this with him. Wanting
this. But she did.

Oh, how she did.

To hell with what she was supposed to do. To hell with
feeling unwanted and unloved and unattractive. What was
she waiting for? *Who* was she waiting for?

Zach made her feel beautiful, desirable. She wanted to keep feeling that way.

When Zach loosened the robe, her heartbeat spiked. But she didn't stop him. She had no intention of stopping him. When would she ever get another chance to feel this way? Eligible men weren't exactly thick on the ground in her grandparents' village.

And even if they were, they'd have been unlikely to risk Salvatore Corretti's wrath by sleeping with his granddaughter out of wedlock.

Zach's warm hand slid along her bare thigh, up beneath the T-shirt he'd loaned her. His touch felt like silk and heat and she only wanted more. She shifted against him, felt the evidence of his arousal. He was hard, thick, and her body reacted with a surge of moisture between her thighs.

A sliver of fear wormed its way through her happiness. Was she really going to do this? Was she really going to have sex for the first time with an American whose last name she didn't even know? Was she going to keep pretending like she knew what she was doing even though she didn't?

Yes.

Yes, most definitely. Today was a new day for Lia Corretti. She was finally going to be brave and decisive and in control of her own destiny. No one would force her to wear an ugly pink dress—or call her fat, mousy and weak—in front of hundreds of people ever again.

The robe fell from her shoulders and then Zach swept her up into his arms. She gasped at his strength as he put a knee on the bed and laid her back on the mattress. And then she froze as he came down on top of her, his jeans-clad body so much bigger than hers.

He must have felt her hesitation because he lifted his head, his dark eyes searching hers. "If you don't want this, Lia—"

She put her fingers over his mouth to stop him from uttering another word. "I do," she said. And then she told a lie. "But it's been a long time and I—I…"

The words died on her lips. Surely he would see right through her, see to the heart of her deception. She had no experience at all, and he would be angry when he figured that out. And then he would send her away.

He pulled her hand from his mouth and pressed a kiss to her palm. "It's been a long time for me, as well." She must have looked doubtful, because he laughed softly. "Cross my heart, Lia. It's the truth."

She lifted a trembling hand to trace her fingers over his firm, sensuous lips. She barely knew him, and yet she felt as if she'd known him forever. But what if she disappointed him somehow? What if this was nothing like she'd read in novels?

"But you are so beautiful," she said.

He laughed, and she realized she'd spoken aloud. Heat flooded her. Oh, how simple she was sometimes!

"And so are you," he said, dipping his head to drop kisses along the column of her throat.

"You don't have to say that." She gasped as his tongue swirled in the hollow at the base of her throat. "I'm already in your bed."

"I never say things I don't mean." He lifted his head, his mouth curling in a wicked grin. "Besides, you're forgetting that I've already seen everything. And I approve, Lia. I definitely approve."

She didn't get a chance to reply because his hands spanned her hips and pushed the T-shirt upward, over her breasts, baring her to his sight.

"Still perfect," he said, and then he took one of her nipples in his mouth, his tongue swirling around the hard little point while she worked so hard not to scream.

She'd had no idea it would feel like this. No idea that a

man's mouth on her breast could send such sweet, aching pleasure shooting into her core. Her sex throbbed with heat and want, and her hands clutched his head, held him to her when she feared he would leave.

He did not. He only moved his attentions to her other breast, and Lia thought she would die from the sensations streaking through her. How had she missed out on this for so many years? How had she missed so much living?

Zach's tongue traced the underside of her breast, and then he was moving down, kissing a hot trail over her stomach. She was torn between anticipation and embarrassment that he could see the soft jiggle of her flesh. Why hadn't she insisted on turning out the light?

But then his tongue slid along the seam of her sex and she forgot everything but him. Lia cried out, unable to help herself. Never had she imagined how good this could feel, how perfect.

He circled her clitoris with his tongue, growing ever closer, until he finally touched her right where all those nerves concentrated. Lia stopped breathing. Her body clenched tighter and tighter as he focused his attention on that single spot. She wanted to reach the peak so badly, and she never wanted it to end, either.

She tried to hold out, tried to make it last, but Zach was far too skilled at making her body sing for him. Lia exploded in a shower of molten sparks, his name on her lips.

She turned her head into the pillow, embarrassed, gasping, trying to gather the shards of herself back together again. What had he done to her? How had he made her lose control so quickly, so thoroughly?

She felt Zach move and she turned to look at him. He stood beside the bed, tugging off his clothes. He looked fierce, and her heart thrummed at the intensity on his face.

She had no idea what she should be doing, but she didn't think she could go wrong by trying to help him remove his clothes. She sat up and started unbuckling his belt while he ripped his shirt over his head.

"Just a minute," he said, turning and disappearing into the adjoining bathroom for a second. When he returned, he was holding a condom package that bore the Corretti Hotel logo. She nearly laughed. Leave it to Matteo to think of everything in his hotels.

Zach's jeans disappeared, and Lia's breath caught at the sheer beauty of his body. He was hard, muscular—but he was also scarred. There was a long red scar that ran along his thigh, and a smaller round scar near his rib cage. Emotion welled inside her as she realized what it was: a bullet wound. She wanted to ask him what had happened, but he knelt between her thighs and rolled on the condom—and all thoughts of bullet wounds fled from her head as her breath shortened at the knowledge of what came next.

He bent and took her mouth with his, stoking the fire inside her instantaneously. When he stretched out over the top of her, she could think of nothing but how perfect this felt, how amazing to be naked beneath a man, his body stretched over hers, dominating hers in all the right ways.

Lia wrapped her legs around his waist, arched her body into him, her hands sliding down his back until she could grip his buttocks. It was natural, instinctual, and she gloried in the sound of approval he made in his throat.

She wanted to explore him, wanted to remember this night forever. But the fire between them was too urgent to go slowly. Lia gasped as she felt the head of his penis at her entrance. She knew this would hurt. What she didn't know was how badly.

Zach reached between them and stroked her. "Are you ready, Lia?" he whispered. "Or have you changed your mind? Last chance to say so."

Lia loved that he would ask. Now, like this, with his body poised to enter hers, he stopped to ask if she still wanted him. Part of her wanted him to stop. Part of her was terrified.

Brave. She nibbled his earlobe between her teeth, felt a ribbon of satisfaction wind through her at the soft growl he emitted. She was brave.

There was no other answer she could give except yes. Her body was on fire, humming from the way he touched her, the way he made her ache for more.

"Please," she said, the only word she could manage. It came out sounding like a sob. Zach stilled for the briefest second—and then he was sliding forward, his body entering hers.

She tensed when there was a slight resistance, but it didn't last. Zach's eyes clouded as he looked down at her, as if he were thinking, but then she shifted her hips, and he groaned softly. He was fully inside her now, his length stretching her in ways she'd never experienced before.

It was the most astonishing feeling. She arched her hips upward, gasping as sensation streaked through her.

"Lia, you make me forget—" She didn't know what else he planned to say because he took her mouth then, kissing her hard, urgently, his tongue sliding against hers so hotly.

They lay like that for a long moment, kissing deeply, their bodies connected and still.

Then he began to move, slowly at first, and then faster as she took everything he had to give and asked for more. The air between them shimmered with heat, with power.

Everything about making love was foreign to her—and yet it wasn't. She felt as if she'd always known how it would be, as if she'd only been waiting for him to take her on this sensual journey.

As they moved together, as their bodies lifted and separated and came together again, she could feel something just out of reach, something wonderful and shattering and necessary. She strained toward it, needing it, trying to catch it—

And then, with a gasp of wonder, she did.

"Yes," he told her, his breath hot in her ear as he threaded his fingers through hers and held her hands over her head, "like that. Just like that, Lia."

Lia sobbed as she flew out over the abyss. And then her breath caught hard in her chest before it burst from her again in a long, loud cry, her senses splintering on the rocks below. Zach captured her mouth, swallowed her cries as she moaned and gasped again and again.

Soon, he followed her over the edge, gripping her hips and lifting her to him as he found his own release. He gave her cries back to her then, and she drank them in greedily, until the only thing that remained was the sound of their breathing.

Zach moved first, lifting himself up and rolling away from her. Lia lay stunned at the intensity of the experience. Like a slow drip from a faucet, uncertainty began to erode the surface of her languor.

What happened now? Did she thank him for the good time, put on the robe and leave? Or did she roll over and run her fingers over the smooth muscle of his abdomen?

She knew what she wanted to do. She wanted to touch him again. Explore him when her body was calm and still.

But she was paralyzed with indecision. And then Zach decided for her. He didn't say anything as he got up and walked into the bathroom. Lia's heart performed a slow dive into her belly. They'd had sex, and he was finished.

She scrambled up and grabbed the robe, slipping it on

and swinging her legs over the side of the bed before he returned. Before she'd gone three steps, he walked out again.

Both of them crashed to a halt, staring at each other.

He was, she thought with a pang, beyond gorgeous. Beautifully, unconsciously naked. Tall and dark, packed with muscle that flexed and popped with his every movement. He looked like something she'd dreamed up instead of a flesh-and-blood man she'd really just had sex with.

Dio, she'd just had sex….

"Zach—"

"Lia—"

They spoke at the same time, their voices clashing. Lia dropped her gaze to the floor.

"Are you hungry?" Zach asked, and she looked up to see him watching her, a half smile on his handsome face. She couldn't keep her eyes from roaming his perfect body, no matter how she tried to focus solely on his face.

"Not that kind of hungry," he added with a laugh. "Though I'm definitely game for another round later."

Another round. Oh, my… Her insides thrummed with electricity at the thought.

"I haven't eaten since breakfast," she managed, her pulse thumping at the idea of doing it all again. And again.

Zach walked over to the desk and picked up the menu there. "Any suggestions?" he asked.

She had to struggle to concentrate. She knew what was on the menu without looking, but she could hardly think of food when Zach stood naked before her.

"Some antipasti, a little pasta alla Norma, some wine. It is all good," she finally managed, knowing that her brother would serve nothing but the best in his hotel.

"And dessert," Zach said, grinning. "Let's not forget dessert." He picked up the phone and ordered in flawless Italian—adding cannoli and fresh strawberries to the list—while Lia went into the bathroom to freshen up.

Her reflection surprised her. She'd thought she would look different—and, indeed, she did in a way. She looked like the cat that'd gotten into the cream. Yes, it was a terrible cliché, but it was truly the best way to describe that look of supreme satisfaction. Her skin glowed and her eyes were bright. Her lips were shockingly rosy and plump.

From kissing Zach. Her stomach flipped hard, and she wondered if she'd be able to eat a bite when he sat there with her, looking so tempting and yummy.

Lia forced herself to focus. She used the comb on the vanity to smooth her wild tangle of hair—as much as possible anyway—and wiped away the mascara that had smudged beneath her eyes. Then, heart pounding, she returned to Zach's suite. He'd pulled on his jeans and sat in a chair by the window, staring at the screen of his smart phone. When he realized she was there, he put the phone on the table.

His gaze was sharp, hot, and her skin began to prickle.

"Your Italian is perfect," she said, casting about for something innocuous to say. Something that would give these butterflies in her belly a chance to settle again. "Where did you learn it?"

"My grandfather was from Sicily," he said. "And I learned it from my mother. She refused to teach me the Sicilian dialect her father spoke, but she did teach me Italian."

Her gaze slid over him again. Now that she knew he had Sicilian blood in him, she could see it. He had the hot, dark eyes of a Sicilian. "Then you have been to Sicily before, yes?"

He inclined his head. "But not for many years."

She went and perched on the edge of the sofa, facing him. His gaze slid over her, warmed her in ways she hadn't known were possible before tonight. "You are friends with the bride's family or the groom's?"

He laughed. "Neither. I came with a friend." He picked up the phone again and frowned as he glanced at the screen. "I can't seem to find her, though."

Her. Lia swallowed as her stomach turned inside out. Of course a man who looked like this one was not alone. But where was his girlfriend, and why hadn't she come searching for him? If it were Lia, she wouldn't let him out of her sight.

But now she needed to do just that. Lia stood. "I should go," she said. "It's late, and you must be tired…."

Words failed her. She turned away, blindly, fighting a sudden rush of ridiculous tears. But then he was there, a hand wrapping around her arm, pulling her back against him so that she could feel the hot press of his body through the robe.

"Forgive me."

"There's nothing to forgive," she said stiffly.

His mouth was on her hair, her temple. "I'm not here with another woman, Lia. Not like that. Taylor is a friend, and she's here to work."

"Taylor Carmichael?" Lia knew of only one Taylor who would be in Sicily to work right now, and that was the gorgeous former child star. She'd heard her grandmother talking about Santo's film, and the troubled woman who was slated to star in it.

She heard Zach sigh. And then he turned her in his arms, put his hands on either side of her face and held her so he could look into her eyes. "Yes, Taylor Carmichael. Yes, she's beautiful and desirable—but not to me. We've only ever been friends. She's the sister I never had."

Lia bit her lip. It was almost impossible to believe that two such gorgeous creatures weren't sleeping together. "I think you need glasses, Zach."

He laughed. "Hardly. I know when I have a beautiful woman in my arms."

Lia flushed with pleasure. She'd never felt beautiful.

Until tonight. Oh, she still worried that she was too fat and too awkward, but she could hardly deny the evidence of his desire for her. She was quite a good dreamer, but she had definitely not dreamed what had happened in his bed only minutes ago.

What she hoped would happen again.

She closed her eyes. One time with him, and she was already becoming a woman of questionable morals.

He tipped her chin up with a long finger and pressed his lips to hers. Desire, so recently sated, still managed to lift a head and send a finger of need sliding down the pathways of her nervous system.

She stepped closer, her lips parting beneath his...and the kiss slid over the edge of polite and into the realm of hot and amazing. He was in the process of shoving the robe off her shoulders when there was a knock on the door.

He took a step back, breaking the kiss, and tugged the robe into place with a sigh of regret. "Food first," he said with a wicked smile. "And then we play."

Lia could only shudder in response.

They spent the night entangled together, their bodies craving the pleasure they found in each other. Lia learned more about sex, about her own body, than she'd dreamed possible.

They showered together in the morning, and then spent the day walking around Palermo, ducking into churches and restaurants, stopping in ancient alleys to kiss and touch, drinking espresso and eating pasta.

It was a perfect day, followed by another perfect evening. They were strangers, and not strangers. It was as if they'd known each other forever. Zach's smile made her heart throb painfully whenever he turned it on her. His laugh had the power to make her ache with raw hunger.

They talked, in Italian and in English, about endless

things. She confessed that she was a Corretti. Zach didn't seem to care, other than a brief lifting of the eyebrows as he connected her to the hotel owners.

She discovered that Zach lived in Washington, D.C., and that he'd met Taylor Carmichael at a clinic for military veterans. She didn't ask about his scars because he'd grown tight-lipped when he'd told her that much.

They returned to the hotel, to his room, and spent the entire night wrapped in each other once more. He left the balcony doors open so that a breeze from the sea blew in. Church bells chimed the hour, every hour, but sanctuary was in this room, this bed.

And yet it was ending. They both knew it. Lia had to return to her grandparents' estate, and Zach was going back to the States. He'd heard from Taylor, finally, and she'd told him everything was fine, though she was somehow now engaged to Lia's brother Luca. Zach didn't seem too happy about that, but he'd accepted it after they'd talked a bit longer.

He did not, Lia noticed, tell Taylor about her.

Yet she kept hoping for more, for some sign this meant more to him than simply sex. It had to. She couldn't be the only one affected by this thing between them. Could she?

But when she awoke early the next morning, Zach was gone. She hadn't heard a thing. His suitcase was gone, everything in the bathroom, everything that indicated he'd once been here.

All that remained was a single rose in a vase and a hastily scribbled note propped beside it. She snatched it up and opened it. The military medal fell out and hit the floor with a plink.

Lia's pulse throbbed as she read the note.

Be well, Lia.

Her heart crumpled beneath the weight of those words. Words that meant well, but ultimately meant nothing. She retrieved the medal, and then sank onto the bed and lifted his pillow to her face. It still smelled like him and she breathed it in, seeking calm.

Zach was gone, and she was alone once more. Like always.

CHAPTER FOUR

THE EVENING WAS hot and muggy, and Zach stood off to one side of the crowd gathered at the country club. He took a sip from his water glass, cleverly disguised as a mixed drink by the addition of a lime slice and a cocktail stirrer, and then set it on a passing tray.

He never drank at functions like this. It was something he'd learned growing up. Always keep your head and always be prepared for any eventuality. His father hadn't made a career in politics out of being imprudent, and Zach had learned the lesson well.

These days, however, he was less concerned with the good impression than he was with the opportunity to escape. Once he'd done his duty—made the speech, shook the hands, accepted the honor, cut the ribbon, got the promised funding for the Scott Foundation's causes—he was gone.

Tonight, he'd had to give a speech. And right now, his father was holding court with a group of people he no doubt hoped would become campaign donors. His mother was circulating with the skill of a career politician's wife, smiling and making polite small talk.

There were reporters in the room—there were always reporters—but the cameras were thankfully stowed at the moment. They'd come out during his speech, of course, and he'd had to work hard to concentrate on the crowd and not the flashes. A matron came over and started to talk to him. He nodded politely, spoke when necessary and kept his eye on the exit. The second he could excuse himself, he was gone. He'd already been here too long, and he was beginning to feel as if the walls were closing in.

He scanned the crowd out of habit, his gaze landing on a woman who made him think of Sicily. She was standing near the door, her head bowed so he couldn't see her face. The crowd moved, closing off his view of her. His pulse started to thrum, but of course, she wasn't Lia Corretti. Lia was in Sicily, no doubt making love to some other lucky bastard. A current of heat slid through him as he remembered her lush body arrayed before him.

If he'd been a different man, he'd have stayed in Sicily and kept her in his bed until they'd grown tired of each other. It's what the old Zach would have done.

But the man he was now couldn't take that chance. He'd spent two nights with her and she'd made him feel almost normal again. Yet it was a lie, and he'd known it.

He didn't know Lia at all, really, but he knew she deserved better than that. Better than him.

"Zach?"

His head whipped around, his gaze clashing with the woman's who'd moved through the crowd unseen and now stood before him. Shock coursed through him. It was as if he'd blinked and found himself whisked back to a different party. Almost against his will, his body responded to the stimulus of seeing her again. He wasn't so inexperienced as to allow an unwanted erection, but a tingle of excitement buzzed in his veins nevertheless.

Lia Corretti gazed up at him, her blue-green eyes filled with some emotion he couldn't place. Her dark red hair was twisted on her head, a few strands falling free to dangle over one shoulder. She was wearing a black dress with high heels and a simple pair of diamond earrings.

She wasn't dripping in jewels like so many of the women in this room, yet she looked as if she belonged. The woman who'd been talking to him had thankfully melted away, her attention caught by someone else.

"Hello, Lia," he said, covering his shock with a blandness that belied the turmoil raging inside him. He spoke as if it hadn't been a month, as if they'd never spent two blissful nights together. As if he didn't care that she was standing before him when what he really wanted to ask her was what the hell she was doing here.

But he was afraid he knew. It wouldn't be the first time a woman he'd slept with had gotten the wrong idea. He was a Scott, and Scotts were accustomed to dealing with fortune hunters. She hadn't seemed to be that type of woman, but clearly he'd been wrong.

He noticed that her golden skin somehow managed to look pale in the ballroom lights. Tight. There were lines around her lips, her eyes. She looked as if she'd been sick. And then she closed her eyes, her skin growing even paler. Instinctively, Zach reached for her arm.

He didn't count on the electricity sizzling through him at that single touch, or at the way she jerked in response.

"I'm sorry," she said in English, her accent sliding over the words. "I shouldn't have come here. I should have found another way."

"Why are you here?" he demanded, his voice more abrupt than he'd intended it to be.

She looked up at him, her eyes wide and earnest. Innocent. Why did he think of innocence when he thought of Lia? They'd had a one-night—correction, two-night—stand, but he couldn't shake the idea that the woman he'd made love to had somehow been innocent before he'd corrupted her.

"I—I need to tell you something."

"You could have called," he said coolly.

She shook her head. "Even if you had given me your number..." She seemed to stiffen, her chin coming up defiantly. "It is not the kind of thing one can say over the phone."

Zach took her by the elbow, firmly but gently, and steered her toward the nearest exit. She didn't resist. They emerged from the crowded ballroom onto a terrace that overlooked the golf course. It was dark, but the putting green was lit and there were still players practicing their swings.

He let her go and moved out of her orbit, his entire body tight with anger and restlessness. "And what do you wish to say to me, Lia?"

He sounded cold and in control. Inhuman. It was precisely what he needed to be in order to deal with her. He'd let himself feel softer emotions when he'd been with her before, and look where that had gotten him. If he'd been more direct, she wouldn't be here now. She would know that her chances of anything besides sex from him were nonexistent.

He would not make that mistake again.

Lia blinked. Her tongue darted out over her lower lip, and a bolt of sensation shot through him at that singular movement. His body wanted to react, but he refused to let it. She was a woman like any other, he reminded himself. If sex was what he wanted, he had only to walk back in that ballroom and select a partner.

Her gaze flicked to the door. "Perhaps we should go somewhere more private."

"No. Tell me what you came to say, and then go back to your hotel."

She seemed taken aback at the intensity of his tone. She ran a hand down her dress nervously, and then lifted it to tuck one of the dangling locks of hair behind her ear. "You've changed," she said.

He shook his head. "I'd think, rather, that you do not know me." He spread his hands wide. "This is who I am, Lia. What I am."

She looked hurt, and he felt an uncharacteristic pinch in his heart. But he knew how to handle this. He knew the words to say because he'd said a variation of them countless times before.

"Palermo was fun. But there can be nothing more between us. I'm sorry you came all this way."

He'd expected her to crumple beneath the weight of his words. She didn't. For a long moment, she only stared at him. And then she drew herself up, her eyes flashing. It was not the response he expected, and it surprised him. Intrigued him, too, if he were willing to admit it.

"There can be more," she said firmly. "There *must* be more."

Zach cursed himself. Why, of all the possible women in the world, had he chosen this one to break his long sexual fast with? He'd known there was something innocent about her, something naive. He should have sent her back to her room. Unfortunately, his brain had short-circuited the instant all the blood that should have powered it started flowing south.

"I'm sorry if you got the wrong idea, sugar," he began.

She didn't let him finish. Her brows drew down angrily as she closed the distance between them and poked him hard in the chest with a manicured finger. He was too stunned to react. "The wrong idea?" she demanded.

She swore in Italian, curses that somehow sounded so pretty but were actually quite rude if translated. Zach was bemused in spite of himself.

"There were consequences to those two days," she flashed. "For both of us, *bello*."

Ice shot down his spine, sobering him right up again.

"What are you talking about?" he snapped.

Her lips tightened. And then she said the words that sliced through him like a sword thrust to the heart.

"I'm pregnant, Zach. With *your* baby."

Lia watched the play of emotions over his face. There was disbelief, of course. Anger. Denial.

She understood all those feelings. She'd experienced each one in the past few days, many times over. But she'd also experienced joy and happiness. And fear. She couldn't forget the fear.

"That's impossible," he said tightly. His handsome face was hard and cold, his eyes like chips of dark, burning ice as they bored into her.

Lia wanted to sit down. She was beginning to regret coming here tonight. She'd only just arrived in Washington today, and she'd hardly rested. She was suffering from the effects of too much air travel, too much stress and too many crazy hormones zinging through her system.

This was not at all how she'd pictured this happening. She hadn't thought beyond seeing him, hadn't thought he would force her to tell him her news standing in the darkness and watching men tap golf balls toward a little hole in the ground.

She also hadn't expected him to be so hostile. So cold.

Lia swallowed against the fear clogging her throat. She had to be brave. She'd already endured so much just to get to this point. There was no going back now.

"Apparently not," she said, imbuing her voice with iron. "Because I am most assuredly pregnant."

"How do you know it's mine?"

His voice was a whip in the darkness, his words piercing her. "Because there has been no one else," she shot back, fury and hurt roiling like a storm-tossed sea in her belly.

"We spent two nights together, Lia. And we used condoms." His eyes were hard, furious.

"There was once," she said, her skin warming. "Once when you, um, when we—"

She couldn't finish the thought. But he knew. He looked stunned. And then he closed his eyes, and she knew he remembered.

"Christ."

There'd been one time when they'd been sleeping and he'd grown hard against her as they slowly wakened. He'd slipped inside her, stroked into her lazily a few times, and then withdrew and put on a condom. It had been so random, so instinctive, that neither of them thought about it afterward.

"Exactly," she said softly, exhaustion creeping into her limbs. Why hadn't she just stayed at the hotel and slept? Her plan had always been to see him privately, but when she'd seen the announcement in the paper about his speech tonight, she'd become focused on getting here and telling him the news. On sharing this burden with someone who could help her.

But that wasn't the only reason.

For an entire month, she'd missed him. Missed his warm skin, the scent of soap and man, the way he skimmed his fingers over her body, the silky glide of his lips against hers.

The erotic pulse of his body inside hers, taking her to heights she'd never before experienced.

Lia shivered, though it was not cold. A drop of sweat trickled between her breasts. She felt…moist. And she definitely needed to sit down.

Zach stood ramrod straight on the terrace before her. "You may be pregnant, but that doesn't make the baby mine," he said. She swallowed down the nausea that had been her constant companion—it was lessening thanks to medication the doctor had prescribed—and tried to bring him into focus. "We were together two nights. How do I know you didn't have another lover?"

Lia's heart ached. She'd known he might not take the news well—what man would when a spontaneous encounter with a stranger turned life-altering in such a huge way?—but she hadn't expected him to accuse her of having another lover. Of basically coming all this way to lie to him.

"I need to get out of this heat," she choked out, turning blindly. She couldn't stand here and defend herself when she just wanted to sit down somewhere cool. When her heart hurt and her stomach churned and she wanted to cry.

She'd only taken a few steps toward the door when she felt as if the bottom was dropping out from under her. Lia shot a hand out and braced herself on the railing near the door as nausea threatened to overwhelm her. She turned to lean against it, grateful for the solid barrier holding her up.

"What's wrong?"

She looked up to find Zach standing over her, his stern face showing concern where moments ago it had only been anger.

Lia put a shaky hand to her forehead. "I'm hormonal, Zach. And you aren't helping matters."

He blew out a breath. And then his hand wrapped around her elbow as he pulled her to his side. "Come on."

He led her away from the door and then in through another door farther down. It led into a dark bar with tables and chairs and only a few patrons. Zach steered her to a table in the corner, far from anyone, and sat her down.

"Wait here."

She was too tired to argue so she did as he ordered, propping her head against one palm as she fought her queasy stomach.

He returned with a glass and a bottle of San Pellegrino, opening it and pouring it for her. She took a grateful sip, let the cold bubbly water slide down her throat and extinguish the fire in her belly.

Zach sank into the chair across from her. His arms were folded over what she remembered was an impressive chest when it was bare. His stare was not in the least bit friendly as he watched her. She thought of the military medal she'd tucked into her purse and pictured him in a flight suit, standing tall and proud beside a sleek fighter jet.

"Better?" he asked shortly.

She nodded. "Somewhat, yes."

"Good." His eyes narrowed. "Why should I believe this baby is mine, Lia?"

Her heart thudded. There was no reason she could actually give him. *Because I was a virgin. Because you are the only man I've ever been with.* "A paternity test should clear it up," she said coolly, though inside she was anything but cool. "I will submit the first moment it is safe to do so."

He turned his head and stared off into space. His profile was sharp, handsome. His hair was still cut in that military style, short and cropped close. On him, it was perfect. Not for the first time, she wondered what he'd seen in her. No doubt he was wondering the same thing.

"You seem to have it all thought out," he said evenly. Coldly.

Lia clutched the glass in her hands. "Not really. All I know is we created a baby together. And our baby deserves to have both parents in his or her life."

It was the one thought that had sustained her on the long trip from Sicily. The one thing she'd had to cling to when everything else was falling apart.

Zach would want his child. She'd told herself that over and over.

But she didn't really know if it was true.

What if he was exactly like her father and just didn't care about the life he'd helped to create? Despair rose up inside her soul. How could this be the same man she'd lain in bed with? That man had been warm, mysterious, considerate. He wouldn't abandon a helpless baby.

But this man...

She shivered. This one was cold and hard and mean.

He looked at her evenly. Across the room, a few people sat at tables or lounged at the bar. One woman leaned in toward the man across from her and said something that made him laugh. How Lia envied that woman. She was with a man who wanted her, a man who was happy she was there.

"I don't know what you expect, Lia, but I'm not the father type. Or the husband type." His voice was low and icy, his emotions so carefully controlled she had no idea if he felt anything at all.

"You don't have a choice about being a father," she said, her throat aching.

His dark eyes glittered. And then he smiled. A cruel smile. "There is always a choice. This is the twenty-first century, not the dark ages. You don't have to have this child. You don't have to keep this child."

His words seared into her. Lia shot to her feet and clutched her tiny purse to her like a shield. Her hands were trembling. Her body was trembling.

"I want this baby, Zach. I intend to give my child the best life possible. With or without you," she added, her throat tightening over the words. Though she didn't know how she was going to do that. She had nothing. The money she had from her mother wasn't in her control. She didn't even know how much there was; her grandfather had always managed it. Now, she supposed, Alessandro was managing it.

She didn't really know Alessandro, but he was her grandfather's handpicked successor. And if he was anything like Salvatore had been, then he was not a man you demanded anything from.

When she walked out of here, she had nothing more than

she'd walked in with. The bit of cash she'd saved from her allowance and the credit card on her grandmother's account. She kept hoping her grandmother wouldn't notice the charges, though she had no idea how much longer that could last. She'd fled while her grandmother was out of town, but Teresa would return any day and find Lia gone.

Then what? The family would shut down her ability to spend a dime other than her cash. Then someone would come for her. Lia shuddered.

Her heart thundered while Zach stared her down. *Please*, she silently begged. *Please don't reject us. Please don't send us back there.*

His eyes did not change. There was no warmth, no sympathy. No feeling at all. She'd been too hasty with that ultimatum. Too stupid.

"Without me," he said, his voice low and measured.

She considered him for a long moment, her eyes pricking with tears, her breath whooshing in and out of her chest as she fought to maintain control. He was a bastard. A horrible, rotten bastard.

What had happened to the man who'd been frightened and alone in that ballroom back in Palermo? The man who'd been vulnerable, and who'd dropped his military medal because he must believe, on some level, that he didn't deserve it?

She'd come here with such hope for the future. She'd come here expecting to find the man who had charmed her and made her feel special.

But this man was not the same man. She despised him in that moment. Despised herself for being so weak and needy that she'd had sex with a stranger—not once, but many times over two days. It was as if she'd wanted to challenge fate, as if she'd been laughing and daring life to knock her in the teeth one more time.

Well, it certainly had, hadn't it? She'd let herself feel

something for a man she didn't know, let herself believe there was more to it than simple biology. Not love, certainly not, but…something. Some feeling that was somehow more than she should have felt for a man she'd only just met.

She was so naive.

The pain sliced into her heart. "I spoke with Taylor Carmichael after you left Sicily. She thinks you are a good man," Lia told him. Something flickered in his gaze, yet he said nothing. "But I think she doesn't really know you the way she thinks she does."

She turned and headed for the exit, though the door was a blur through her tears. One of the patrons in the bar looked up as she passed. He grinned at her, an eyebrow lifting, but she kept walking, her entire world crumbling apart. She hoped Zach would stop her. Prayed he would.

Prayed that she was wrong and he was just very surprised and not reacting well.

But she reached the door and tugged it open, and still he wasn't behind her. Lia stepped into the corridor and hurried down it, her heels sinking into the plush carpet. And then she was outside, nodding to the doorman's query if she would like a taxi. Here, the world moved as it had before. Nothing had changed. Inside her soul, however, everything was different.

She was pregnant. She was alone.

She wished she had someone to talk to—a friend, a sister, anyone who would listen—but that was wishful thinking. She'd never had anyone to talk to.

A taxi glided up the rounded drive and the doorman opened it with a flourish. Lia handed him a few dollars and then slid inside and turned her head away from the elegant building as the taxi drove away. She refused to look back. That part of her life was over.

CHAPTER FIVE

LIA DIDN'T SLEEP well. She'd returned to her hotel, ordered room service—soup and crackers—and then taken a hot bath and climbed into bed with the television remote. She'd fallen asleep almost instantly, but then she'd awakened when it was still dark out. She lay there and stared at the ceiling.

Her entire life was crashing around her ears, and there was nothing she could do about it. Zach had rejected her. She had no choice but to return to Sicily. No choice but to tell her grandmother everything that had happened. She could only pray that Alessandro was a better man than her grandfather had been, and that he wouldn't force her to marry someone she didn't love simply for the sake of protecting the family reputation

She didn't hold out much hope, actually.

She put her hand over her still-flat belly. What was she going to do? Where was she going to go? If she tried to keep running, the Correttis would find her. She couldn't melt away and become anonymous. She couldn't find a job and raise her child alone. She had no idea how to begin. She had no skills, no advanced education. She'd never worked a day in her life.

But she would. She would, damn it, if that's what it took. She wasn't half-bad with plants. Maybe she could get a job in a nursery, or in someone's garden. She could prune plants, coax forth blooms, mulch and pot and plan seasonal beds.

It wasn't much, but it was something.

Tears filled her eyes and she dashed them away angrily. Eventually, she fell asleep again. When she woke this time, it was full daylight. She got up and dressed. She thought about ordering room service again, but she needed to be careful with her expenses. She would go and find a diner somewhere, a place she could eat cheaply.

And then she would figure out what to do.

Lia swept her long hair into a ponytail and grabbed her purse. She was just about to open the door when someone knocked on it. The housekeeper, no doubt. She pulled open the door.

Except it wasn't the housekeeper.

Lia's heart dipped into her toes at the sight of Zach on the threshold. But then it rose hotly as anger beat a pulse through her veins. He'd been so cruel to her last night.

"What do you want?" she asked, holding the door tight with one hand. Ready to slam it on him.

"To talk to you."

He was so handsome he made her ache. And that only made her madder. Was she really such a pushover for a pretty face? Was that how she'd found herself in this predicament? The first man to ever pay any real attention to her had the body of a god and the face of an angel—was it any wonder she'd fallen beneath his spell?

This time she would be strong. She gripped the door hard, her knuckles whitening. "I understood you the first time. What more can you have to say?"

He blew out a breath, focused on the wall of windows behind her head. "I called Taylor."

Her heart throbbed with a new emotion. Jealousy. "And this concerns me how?"

"You know how, Lia. Let me in so we can talk."

She wanted to say no, wanted to slam the door in his

face—but she couldn't do it. Wordlessly, she pulled the door open. Then she turned her back on him and went over to the couch to sit and wait. He came inside and stood a few feet away, his hands shoved into his jeans pockets.

"You went to see Taylor," he said. "To find out where I lived."

She lifted her chin. "I knew you lived in Washington, D.C. You told me so."

"Yes, but it's a big city. And you needed an address."

She toyed with the edge of her sleeve. "I'd have found you. You did tell me about your father, if you recall."

But it would have been much harder, which was why she'd gone to see Taylor. And how embarrassing that had been. She'd had to explain to a complete stranger that she needed to find Zach because she had something to tell him.

Taylor hadn't accepted that excuse. She'd demanded to know more. Lia hadn't blamed her, since she was Zach's friend, but it was still a humiliating experience. Taylor hadn't actually believed her—until she'd produced the medal. Lia still wasn't certain that Taylor believed everything, but she'd relented at that point because she'd believed enough.

"You've gone to a lot of trouble," he said.

Lia swallowed. What could she say? *I had no choice? My family will be furious? I'm afraid?*

"A baby needs two parents," she said. "And a man should know if he's going to be a father."

"And just what did you expect me to do about it, sugar?"

Irritation zipped through her like a lash. *Sugar* wasn't an endearment, spoken like this; it was a way of keeping her at a distance. Of objectifying her. "You know my name. I'd prefer you use it."

His eyes flashed. "Lia, then. Answer the question."

She folded her arms and looked toward the windows. She could see the white dome of the Capitol building sitting on the hill. Why had she chosen this hotel? It was far too expensive. If her grandmother cut off her credit cards, she'd be doing dishes in the hotel kitchen for the next ten years just to pay for one night.

"I thought you would want to know."

"You could have called."

She swung back to look at him. "Are you serious? Would you want this kind of news over the phone?"

He didn't answer. Instead, he pulled something from his rear pocket and tapped it on his palm. "How much money do you want, Lia?"

Her heart turned to stone in her chest as she realized he was holding a checkbook. And though she needed money—desperately—it hurt that he thought all he needed to do was buy her off.

And it hurt that he didn't want this child growing inside her. That he could so easily shove aside that connection and have nothing to do with a person who was one half of him.

My God, she'd really chosen well, hadn't she?

"You think I came here for money?" It would solve her most immediate problem, but it wouldn't really solve anything. She'd still be single and pregnant, and her family would still be furious—and the Correttis had a long arm.

"Didn't you?"

Lia stood. She had to fold her arms over her middle to hide their trembling. "Get out," she said, fighting the wave of hysteria bubbling up inside her.

He took a step toward her and then stopped. The checkbook disappeared in his jeans again. He looked dark and broody and so full of secrets he frightened her. And yet a part of her wanted, desperately, to slide into his arms and experience that same exhilaration she had back in Sicily.

"You expect marriage," he said, almost to himself. "That's why you came."

It seemed so silly when spoken aloud like that, but she couldn't deny the truth of it. She had thought she would race to D.C., tell Zach she was pregnant and he would be so happy he'd want to take care of her and the baby forever.

Lia closed her eyes. What was wrong with her? Why was she always looking for acceptance and affection where there was none? Why did she think she needed a man, any man, in her life anyway?

"This is your baby in here," she said, spreading her hand over her abdomen. "How can you not want it?"

He raked a hand through his hair and turned away from her. Once more, she was studying his beautiful, angry profile.

"Assuming what you say is true, I'm not good father material." He said it quietly, with conviction, and her heart twisted in her chest.

Still, she couldn't allow sympathy for the pain in his voice to deflect her from the other part of what he'd said. "If you don't believe me, why are you here? Do you usually offer to pay women to get them to go away?"

He turned back to her, his expression cool. "I've encountered this situation before, yes. It has never been true, by the way." He spread his hands wide. "But my family name encourages the deception."

Lia stiffened. "I really don't care who your family is," she said tightly. "I did not come here for them."

"Then what do you want, Lia?"

She swallowed. She'd thought—naively, of course—there had been something between them in Palermo. Something more than just simple animal attraction. She'd thought he might be glad to see her. God, she was such a fool.

The only thing she had was the truth.

"My family will be very angry when they find out," she said softly. "And Alessandro will likely marry me off to one of his business associates to prevent a scandal." She dropped her gaze and smoothed her hand over her belly again. "I suppose I could deal with that if it were only me. But I'm afraid for my baby. A Sicilian man won't appreciate a wife who is pregnant with another man's child."

She could feel his gaze on her and she lifted her head, met the tortured darkness of his eyes. And the heat. It surprised her to find heat there, but it was indisputable. The heat of anger, no doubt.

"You know this to be true," she said. "You are part Sicilian yourself."

"A small part, but yes, I know what you mean."

She could have breathed a sigh of relief—except she didn't think he'd changed his mind about anything. "Then you will not want your child raised by another man. A man who will not love him or her, and who will resent the baby's presence in his household."

Zach was still. "You should have chosen better," he said.

She blinked. It was not at all the response she'd anticipated. "I beg your pardon?"

"That night. You should have chosen to leave instead of stay."

She'd bared her fears to him and this was what he had to say. Anger spiked in her belly. "It takes two, Zach. You were there, too."

He took a step toward her, stopped. His hands flexed at his sides. "Yes, and I tried to send you away, if you will recall. Considering how we first met, you should have run far and fast."

Her skin was hot—with shame, with anger, with self-recrimination. "It's not all my fault. Perhaps you should have tried harder."

As if anything would have induced her to leave after the way he'd looked at her: as if he wanted to devour her. It had been such a novel experience that she'd only wanted more.

"I should have," he said. "But I was weak."

"This baby is yours," she said, a thread of desperation weaving through her. If he walked out now, if he sent her back to Sicily, what would become of her and the baby? She couldn't face her cousin's wrath. Her grandmother would do what she could, but even Teresa Corretti would do what the head of the family dictated in the end. And he would dictate that she not have a child out of wedlock. Or he would throw her out and cut her off without a cent.

For a moment, she contemplated that option. It would be…heavenly, in a way. She would be free of the Correttis, free of the pain and anger that went along with being the outsider in her family.

Except she knew it wouldn't happen that way. Salvatore Corretti had ruled his family with an iron fist. And no wayward granddaughter would have ever brought shame on the family name in such a way. A Corretti grandson could father illegitimate children all day long, and he would not have cared. Let one of his granddaughters get pregnant, with no man in sight, and he most certainly would have come unglued.

Alessandro was a Corretti male and would be no different. He'd learned at their grandfather's knee how to run this family and she could not take the risk he was somehow more enlightened. He'd never been enlightened enough to pay attention to her in all these years, which told her a lot about how he already felt about her. Add in the humiliation of his aborted wedding, and she was certain he was in no mood to be sympathetic.

"How can you be sure, Lia?"

She had to give herself a mental shake to retrieve the thread of the conversation. He wanted to know how she could be sure the baby was his, as if she was the kind of woman who had a different sexual partner every night.

"Because I am. Because I've been with no one else."

He swore softly.

Her cheeks heated. Hot emotion whipped through her. She was tired of feeling guilty, tired of feeling as if she was the one who'd done something wrong. She felt snappish.

"This isn't ideal for me, either, you know. I didn't ask to get pregnant, especially not my first time ever having sex—"

She broke off as she realized what she'd said. His face grew thunderous. He closed the distance between them, stopped just short of grabbing her. His hands were clenched into fists at his sides. "What did you say?"

Lia's heart pounded. Adrenaline roared through her veins. She felt light-headed. "Nothing," she whispered as his eyes darkened. "It was nothing."

"You told me that night it had been a long time...." His voice was diamond-edged.

"I thought if I told you the truth, you'd send me away."

He swallowed, hard. "I would have. I should have anyway." His gaze dropped, his dark lashes dipping to cover his beautiful eyes. "I thought something was...different with you. But it had been so long since I'd been with anyone that I dismissed my intuition. You didn't act like a virgin, but you felt like one when I..."

He swore again, his eyes meeting hers once more. "I'd have done things differently if I'd known. Been more gentle. You should have told me."

Lia couldn't stop herself from lifting a hand and sliding it along the bare skin of his arm. It was the first time she'd touched him, really touched him, in a month. And the electric sizzle ricocheting through her body told her just how little had changed for her.

"I should have. I know it. But everything was so surreal, and I was afraid it would end. You were the first person to make me feel wanted in a very long time. I liked that feeling."

He moved away from her, went over and sank down on a chair. Then he sat forward and put his head in his hands. Lia didn't say anything. She didn't move, though her heart throbbed at the sight of him looking so overwhelmed.

"This is not what I expected to happen at this point in my life," he said to the floor.

"I don't think either of us did," she replied, swallowing. "And though I could make it all go away with a visit to a doctor, as you intimated earlier, I can't do that. It's not who I am or what I want."

He lifted his head. "No, I know that." He blew out a breath, swore. And then he stood again, his presence nearly overwhelming her as his eyes flashed fire. "The press will have a field day with this."

Lia bit the inside of her lip. In all the drama, she'd never considered the press. It was true the paparazzi flocked around her family like piranha. But she'd never been their target, probably because she was so humdrum and uninteresting in her family of brilliant swans.

But this baby was a game changer, especially considering who Zach was. His family was even more famous than hers. American royalty, if there was such a thing. A family with incredible wealth and power. She'd read all about the Scotts on her way across the Atlantic.

And she'd read about their heroic son, a man who'd returned from the war after a dramatic plane crash behind enemy lines. Her gaze drifted to where she'd set her purse. Inside, in a little zippered pocket, she still had Zach's medal. A medal he hadn't cared about.

She thought of him flat against the ballroom wall in the Corretti Hotel, his eyes tightly closed as he fought against something, and knew there was more to the story than had been reported.

"We're the only ones who know," she said. "And I have no plans to inform them. I think the secret is safe for now."

His gaze was steady, cool, and she realized he didn't entirely trust her. It stung.

"There are always leaks." He shoved a hand through his hair. "There's only one way to deal with this. One way to keep everything from exploding into an even bigger problem than it already is."

Her heart thundered in her chest. And it hurt, too. Hurt because he'd called her—and their baby—a problem.

"Congratulations, Lia," he said, his voice chilling her. "You've won the jackpot, after all. You're about to become a Scott."

"This is not how I wanted this to happen," she said on a throat-aching whisper. Tears pressed the backs of her eyes. She couldn't let them fall.

"You came here," he said, his voice hard. "What did you expect? Did you think I would be happy?"

She dropped her gaze. A single tear spilled free and she dashed it away, determined not to cry in front of him. Not to be weak.

"I had hoped you might be, yes." She lifted her chin and sucked back her tears. "Clearly, I was mistaken."

"We'll marry," he said. "Because we must. But it's an arrangement, do you understand? We'll do it for as long as necessary to protect our families, and then we'll end it when the time comes."

Anger started to burn in her, scouring her insides. He was no better than her father had been. He didn't care about his child any more than Benito Corretti had cared about her. He was making a deal, nothing more. It made her sick. And furious.

"Fine," she said tightly. "I accept. But if we are having an arrangement, as you so nicely put it, then I want it understood that this arrangement is in name only."

She didn't know what made her say that, but once she said it she knew it was right. Because this situation was so out of her power that she needed something she could control. Something she could have a say about.

He stared at her for a long moment. And then his sexy lips curled up in a smile, surprising her after he'd been so hard and cold. "I can't guarantee that, sugar. But we'll try it your way to start. Just know that when you do surrender to me, I won't be saying no."

Lia pulled herself erect and looked at him with all the haughtiness she could muster. Which wasn't much, she was sure. But damn if he hadn't infuriated her. "There will be no surrender, Zach. Not ever again."

"We'll see," he said with all the arrogant surety of a man who was accustomed to getting his way. And then he headed toward the door. "I'll let you know when the arrangements are made."

"How long will this take?" she asked as he opened the door.

He turned back to her. "Eager, Lia?"

She sucked in a breath. No, she was just worried about her ability to stay in this hotel. And about her family sending someone to fetch her if they figured out where she was. "No, but I have no idea how long these things take in America. I can't stay in this hotel for weeks, Zach."

His eyes slipped over her. "No, you can't. The media will descend soon enough. You'll move in with me. I'll send someone for you later."

He closed the door before she could say another word. She

stood there for a long time, uncertain whether she'd found salvation by coming to D.C.

Or whether she'd damned herself instead.

CHAPTER SIX

ZACH LIVED IN a sprawling house in Virginia. It was gated, with manicured green lawns and a view of the Potomac River. Here, the Potomac was still close to the source and was wilder and freer than it had been in Washington. It tumbled over huge boulders, rushing and gurgling toward the city where it would become wide, placid and subject to Chesapeake tides.

Lia stood in a room that overlooked the backyard and the cliffs of the Potomac. Glass doors opened onto a wide stone balcony that ran the length of the house. Immediately outside was a small seating area, with a chair and a table. Perfect for reading.

The gardens weren't overly ornate, but there were a lot of gorgeous flowering plants in manicured beds. Roses bloomed in profusion along two stone walls, red and pink and white. Fat flowering hydrangeas, blue and pink, sat in the shade beneath tall trees, and a host of bright annuals bloomed in beds that ran down toward the river.

Lia's fingers itched. She wanted to lose herself in the garden, to go dig into the dirt and forget all about Zach Scott and the Correttis for a while.

But that was impossible right now.

She hadn't seen Zach since she'd arrived. A chauffeur had come to get her at the hotel earlier, after a terse call from

Zach informing her to be ready. Once she'd arrived, a uniformed maid had showed her to this room and offered to put her things away. Lia only had one suitcase and a carry-on, so she didn't really have much with her. She'd declined and hung everything herself.

Now she felt like she was in stasis. Just waiting for something to happen. The garden called to her, but she resisted. What would Zach think if he came looking for her and she was on her knees in the dirt?

As the minutes dragged by, she resolved to go out on the balcony and run her fingers through the potted geraniums and lavender, just for something to do, but a knock at her door stopped her. "Yes?" she called.

The door opened and Zach stood there, tall, handsome and brooding as ever. Lia folded her arms over her chest and waited.

"If you've no objection, I've brought a doctor who is going to take a blood sample."

"Why?"

Zach came into the room, his hands shoved into the pockets of his faded jeans. *Dio*, he was sexy. Lia shook herself and tried not to think about him that way. She failed, naturally. Her heart thumped and pumped and her bones loosened in the shell of her skin.

"There is a paternity test that will isolate the baby's DNA from your blood. Just to be certain, you realize."

Lia lifted her chin. "I have nothing to hide."

It hurt, of course, that he didn't believe her. But if a test would erase all doubt, she was for it. Not only that, but she also looked forward to the apology he would have to make when the test proved he was this baby's father.

"I'll bring her up, then."

"Yes, do."

He left and then returned a few minutes later with a smiling woman who took Lia's blood and asked her questions about how she was feeling. Once it was over, and the woman was gone, Lia was left with Zach.

"I have an important dinner to attend tonight," he told her. "You will accompany me."

Lia swallowed. She wasn't accustomed to large gatherings. Aside from the wedding-that-wasn't, and a few family things that happened once a year, she spent most of her time alone or with her grandmother.

"I don't have anything to wear," she said. She didn't even know what kind of dinner it was, but if it was anything like that gathering she'd crashed last night, she knew she didn't have anything appropriate. She'd put on the nicest thing she had for that event.

Zach didn't look perturbed. "There is time. I'll send you to my mother's personal shopper."

"That is not necessary," she said, though in truth she wouldn't begin to know where to start in this city.

"I think it is, Lia. It'll go much faster if you simply let her help you pick out what you need. For tonight, you'll need formal wear. But select a range of clothing appropriate for various events."

"And do you attend many events?" she asked, her heartbeat spiking at the thought of being out among so many people so frequently.

Plants she understood. People not so much.

His eyes were flat. "I am a Scott. And a returning war hero. My presence is in demand quite often, I'm afraid."

She didn't miss the way his voice slid over the words *war hero*. It was like they were oily, evil words for some reason. As if he hated them.

"You don't sound as if you enjoy it."

One corner of his mouth lifted. "No, I don't. Not anymore."

She wanted to ask what had changed, but she didn't. "Then why do it?"

"Because I am a Scott. Because people depend on me. And if you are going to be a Scott, too, then you'd better get used to doing things because you have to instead of want to."

Lia nibbled the inside of her lip. She was no good at the social thing. She had no practice at it. But, for tonight, she would have to try and be something she wasn't. She would have to navigate the social waters without falling flat on her metaphorical face.

"I'm no good at this, Zach," she told him truthfully. "I don't have any experience."

Not to mention she was awkward and grew tongue-tied around too many people. She'd always been so self-conscious, so worried about whether or not others liked her.

Because she'd never felt very wanted and she didn't know how to fix it.

"Then you'll learn," he said. "Because you have no choice."

Zach slipped into his tuxedo jacket and tugged the cuffs of his shirt until they were straight beneath the jacket arms. Tonight was another event, another speech, where he would be speaking to some of Washington's elite about the need for funding for veterans' causes. Everyone tended to think, because the military worked for the government, that returning vets' care was assured. It was to a point. Where that point ended was where Zach stepped in.

But tonight was different in a way he had not expected. For the first time since he'd returned from the war, he was taking a woman with him. A woman who was his date.

His fiancée, for God's sake. An unsettled feeling swirled in his gut at the notion, but it was too late to back out now.

He'd had the call from the doctor. They'd rushed the re-sults—because he'd paid them a great deal of money to do so—and he knew the truth.

Lia Corretti was pregnant with his child.

He wasn't quite sure how that made him feel. He was still stunned at his reaction to her earlier today, in her hotel room, when he'd suddenly decided that marrying her was the thing to do. It had been a preemptive strike, because though he'd fully intended to get an answer to the child's paternity be-fore proceeding, he'd also known on a gut level that she was telling him the truth.

She'd been a virgin. He'd realized something was dif-ferent about her that night in Palermo, but she'd distracted him before he'd puzzled out precisely what it was. Not that being a virgin made someone truthful, but he imagined it was highly unlikely she'd turned around and taken a new lover so quickly.

His gut had known what his head hadn't wanted to admit. And now he had a fiancée. A fiancée he didn't quite know how to fit into this life of his. She hadn't wanted to accom-pany him tonight, but he'd insisted she would anyway.

He'd been angry and resentful toward her all day. But now he felt a twinge of guilt over his reaction. Still, he'd told her the truth. She would learn to deal with her responsibilities as his wife because she had no choice.

They had appearances to maintain and commitments to keep. If he was going to have a wife, then she was going to be at his side. It's the way it worked in his world. The way it had always worked.

He went downstairs and into his office, where he opened the wall safe and extracted a box. He'd told Lia to shop for clothing, but he'd not thought of jewelry. He had no idea what she would wear tonight, but he knew what would look good with her coloring. He opened the box and slid a finger over the art deco rubies and diamonds. These had belonged to his grandmother. She'd left them to him on her death and he'd put them away, certain it would be years before he found a woman to give them to.

He flipped the box closed after a long moment and held it tight. His life was changing in ways he hadn't expected. Ways he wasn't quite sure how to cope with. He resented the changes, but he would deal with them the way he dealt with everything else in his life these days.

By hiding his feelings beneath a mountain of duty and honor.

She was learning, or trying to. Lia stood beside Zach at a posh gathering being held in the National Gallery of Art. It was past closing time, and the museum was only open for this exclusive party.

She'd chosen a gown in a rich cream color, and swept her dark hair off her shoulders and pinned it up. She'd applied her makeup carefully, slid into her heels—not too high because she was already self-conscious about her height—and wrapped a shawl around her shoulders. Her jewelry had consisted of her simple diamonds, until she'd arrived downstairs and found Zach waiting for her in the foyer of the big house.

His gaze had flicked over her appreciatively, and she'd felt warmth spread through her limbs. She liked the way he looked at her. And she wasn't happy about that. After the way he'd behaved since she'd arrived, she didn't want to like anything about him. She kept telling herself that the man she'd spent two days with was gone—except she couldn't quite convince herself when he looked at her the way he had earlier.

"Wear these," he'd said, flipping open a box that held a

ruby-and-diamond necklace and matching earrings. It was ornate, but somehow simple, too. An impressive feat for an expensive necklace.

"I shouldn't," she said. "I'm too clumsy—"

"Nonsense." His tone had been firm. "You're a beautiful woman, Lia. And you are about to be my wife."

He'd taken the necklace from the box and clasped it on her once he'd removed her small pendant. Then he placed her necklace carefully in the box he'd taken the larger necklace from. She was grateful for that, considering it was the only jewelry she had that had belonged to her mother. It might be small and unimpressive, but Zach didn't treat it that way, and that touched her even though she did not want it to. He held out his hand for her earrings, which she handed over, and then she put the diamonds and rubies on.

When she was finished, he gave a satisfactory smile. "Excellent. You look lovely."

They'd climbed into the Mercedes, and the chauffeur—Raoul—had driven them here, where Zach had been greeted like the political royalty he was. Now, they were sipping cocktails and waiting for the dinner to begin.

She didn't miss that women slanted their gazes toward her. Some were appraising while others were downright hostile. Zach kept her at his side. Periodically, he would drape an arm around her, or slide his hand into the small of her back to guide her through the crowd. His touches made her jumpy yet she found herself craving them.

Soon they were seated at a large round table toward the front of the gathering. Lia wasn't intimidated by the array of cutlery and plates before her. She might not be any good at the socializing part of this, but she'd been brought up by Teresa Corretti, the most elegant woman in all of Sicily. Lia knew which fork to use, and which bread plate was hers.

She also knew how to sit through a multicourse meal and how to pace herself so that she wasn't too full before the last course arrived.

But tonight she was finding it hard to concentrate on her food. She was still tired from the trip, and the stress of everything was starting to overwhelm her. She'd left Sicily on impulse, and now she was here with Zach, and he wasn't the man she'd thought he was.

He was an automaton, an aristocrat, a man who did what he had to do because he cared about things like social standing and reputation. While it wasn't a foreign concept to her, coming from the Corretti family, it wasn't what she'd thought she was fleeing toward when leaving Sicily.

She could hardly reconcile the man he was here—dressed in a bespoke tuxedo and sporting an expensive watch—with the stiff military man who'd thrown a medal at her feet. The two did not seem to go together, and it confused her.

"You aren't eating."

His breath ghosted over her ear and a shiver of something slid down her backbone. She turned her head, discovered that he was frowning down at her, his dark eyes intense.

"I'm tired," she said. "My schedule is all messed up. In a couple of hours, I would be waking up and having breakfast, were I still home."

"You need to eat something. For your health."

She knew what he meant. And why he didn't say it. "I've eaten the soup and some of the bread."

"Beef is good for you. There's iron in there."

"I've had a bite of it."

"Eat more, Lia."

"I can't eat just because you order me to," she snapped quietly.

Zach glanced at someone across the table and smiled.

Then he lifted his hand and slid it along her jaw, turning her head as he did so. To anyone else, the gesture looked loving and attentive. But she knew what it really was. He was attempting to keep her in line.

His eyes held hers. She couldn't look away. His mouth was only inches away, and she found herself wanting to stretch toward him, wanting to tilt her face up and press her lips to his.

His gaze dropped to her mouth, and one corner of his beautiful, sensual lips lifted. "Yes, precisely," he murmured. She felt her face flood with heat. "And I am not ordering you to eat, Lia. I'm concerned about your health."

She dropped her gaze from his. "*Grazie*. But I will not let my health suffer, I assure you."

"Excellent," he said. "Because you are mine now, and I take care of what is mine."

A shiver slid through her. And a flash of anger. "Are you certain about that? What if the test results aren't what you want them to be?"

His eyes sparkled with humor that she sensed was at her expense. "I've already had the result. And it is precisely what you said it was."

Lia wanted to jerk herself out of his grip, but she knew this was not the place to show a bit of temper. "You could not have told me this earlier?"

He shrugged. "Why? You already knew the answer."

"Perhaps I would like an apology. You did suggest I was lying, as well as exceedingly promiscuous."

"My mistake."

"You consider that an apology?"

"I do. You must realize, sugar, that you aren't the first to try and trap me this way. You're just the first to succeed."

Lia shoved her chair back, uncaring how it looked to the other guests at their table. The murmur of conversation ceased and all eyes were on her. She swallowed and stood, hoping the trembling didn't show.

"If you will excuse me, ladies and gentlemen," she said. "I believe I must freshen up."

Then she turned and marched away without waiting for a response. She was certain the fashionable ladies were appalled with her. The gentlemen probably shrugged it off as foreign eccentricity. Nevertheless, she didn't quite care what they thought. She wasn't about to sit there and let Zach talk to her like that.

She found the ladies' room and went inside to perch on one of the settees and calm down. She refreshed her lipstick in the mirror and smoothed a few stray hairs into place. As she gazed at her reflection, it hit her how unusual her reaction just now had been. She'd sat through enough humiliating Corretti functions in her life to know how to be invisible for the duration.

She also knew how to be a lady whenever any attention happened to turn on her, and she knew that marching away in a huff was not a part of the training her grandmother had instilled in her. Teresa Corretti would be disappointed at that display of temper just now.

Lia curled her hands into fists on her lap and took a deep breath. Damn Zach, he had a way of getting beneath her skin and irritating her so much that she simply reacted without thinking. It wasn't like her to draw attention to herself, or to argue, but she couldn't help it with him.

Still, she should not have let him get to her like that. But he'd suggested she'd purposely set out to trap him into marriage, and it made her furious. What kind of God's gift to women did he think he was anyway? It was ludicrous. And she planned to tell him so just as soon as they were alone and she could give him a proper piece of her mind.

Lia stood and smoothed her dress. She studied herself in the mirror and was pleased with what she saw. Oh, she was still too plump—and too tall—but she cleaned up quite nicely when she was able to wear designer dresses someone had picked out specifically for her shape and coloring.

When she left the ladies' room, Zach was standing across from the door, leaning against the wall in a sexy slouch that made her heart kick up. He really was spectacular. Tall, broad and intensely handsome. The kind of man that, yes, would have women falling all over him.

"You've been gone awhile," he said.

Lia tilted her chin up. "Yes. I needed to get my temper under control."

Zach laughed. She didn't like the way the sound slid beneath her skin. Curled around her heart. Warmed her from the inside out.

"I wasn't aware you had a temper, Lia."

"Of course I do. And you know just how to aggravate it." She'd never really realized precisely how furious another person could make her until she'd met Zach. He had an ability to make her feel things she'd never quite felt before—and to say things she would have never said to another person. Usually, she hid her emotions down deep.

Except with him. With him, she couldn't help but say what she was feeling.

It was that or burst.

She crossed the hall and stood right in front of him, nearly toe to toe. She was tall in her heels, five-eleven, but she still had to tilt her head back to look up at him. "You might think you are some sort of priceless gift to womankind, Zach Scott, but I'll have you know that I would much prefer to be back home and for none of this to have happened."

It wasn't quite true, but she wasn't going to tell him that.

She wasn't sorry for the two nights they'd spent together. She wasn't even sorry about her baby. She was sorry for the way it had happened, and for the man it had happened with. Why couldn't she have chosen a good Sicilian man for her night of rebellion? A single, sexy Sicilian who had no hang-ups about women and their motives.

Even as she thought it, she knew she didn't really want that, either.

"For your information," she continued, "I did not set out to 'trap' you. That is the most arrogant, conceited, unbelievable thing you have said yet. No one forced you to do what you did in Palermo. No one forced you to take that risk."

His expression was dark. "No, you're right about that. No one forced me. It was a mistake, and I was stupid enough to make it." His eyes slid over her, came to rest on her face again. "Everything about those two days was a mistake."

Lia tried not to let that hurt her, but she didn't quite succeed. It stung her in places she'd thought she'd locked away long ago. "Well, now that we have that out of the way, I think it must be time for the dessert course."

She turned her back on him and started down the hall, back toward the dinner. Tears pricked her eyes. Angry tears, she told herself.

Zach's hand on her elbow brought her up short. She whirled around and jerked out of his grip.

He was a dark, brooding presence. "Look, I didn't mean that the way it sounded." He shoved a hand through his hair, blew out a breath.

Lia glared at him steadily. "I did not trap you, Zach. I'd like you to admit that."

His expression remained dark. "Fine. You didn't trap me."

"And what about not believing I was telling the truth? Are you going to admit you were wrong about that, too?"

His eyes gleamed. "No."

She stiffened. "Of all the rude, arrogant—"

"What reason did I have to believe you?" he said heatedly. "We're strangers, Lia, regardless of what happened in Palermo."

She swallowed against the knot of anger and pain clogging her throat. But she knew what he said was true. Would she have believed a story like hers if she were Zach? Considering his previous experience of women, perhaps not.

"I will concede that point," she said coolly, though her heart beat hot at the admission. "But I don't like it."

He reached for her hand, slipped it into his. Her entire body went on red alert just from that simple touch. She wanted more of him, more of what they'd had in Palermo. And yet she knew that was the last thing she should want. The very last. They had an arrangement in name only, to protect their families, until such time as they could go their separate ways and not cause a scandal.

She had to remember he didn't truly want this child. Or her.

She tried to pull her hand away, but he held it tight.

"Darling, we're returning to the event," he chided her. "We have to look happy together if they are to believe our whirlwind romance."

"I'm not very good at pretending," she said stiffly.

He tugged her closer. "Then I will have to give you a reason to smile," he said, slipping his hand around to the small of her back and pressing her against him. He pulled the hand he'd trapped up to his chest, pressed her palm against the smooth fabric of his tuxedo.

"There is nothing you can do to make me smile, Zach," she said, though her heart beat harder and faster as the look in his eyes changed. Heat flared in their dark depths and her body responded by softening, melting. She held herself rigid, unwilling to give in to the feelings swirling inside her. Feelings that wanted her to tilt her head back and offer her lips up for him to claim. "I want you to let me go."

His eyes were hooded as they dropped to her mouth, and a shot of adrenaline pulsed into her veins.

"I will," he murmured. "But not quite yet."

CHAPTER SEVEN

ZACH WAS ON the edge of control. Not in a way that made him sweat as helpless panic rose in his throat and threatened to squeeze the life from him. But he had a need to dominate. A need to take this infuriating woman to his bed and not let her out of it for several hours.

Not until she sighed her pleasure into his ear. Not until she gasped out his name the way she had in Palermo. Sweet, innocent Lia. He wanted to taste her again. Wanted to know if she was as sweet as he remembered. As intoxicating.

She stood very still in his grasp. He didn't hold her tight. She could have broken free with a single tug. Oh, not when he'd first gripped her hand. Definitely not then. At that moment, he'd been intending to saunter back into the gathering with his woman at his side, looking happy and enraptured for the world to see.

He knew how this game was played. He could have a fast romance and marriage, but first he had to be seen with Lia. And they needed to appear as if they couldn't keep their hands off each other. So far, they'd looked as if they might prefer to touch anyone else rather than each other.

He had to change that perception, especially since there were at least three reporters circulating at this party tonight. Tomorrow, on the society pages of the local papers, they'd mention his date. By tomorrow evening, they'd know everything about Lia Corretti.

And what he wanted them to know was that she was mad for him.

Except she didn't look so much mad for him as mad at him at the moment. Furious, with her snapping blue-green eyes and dark auburn hair that caught the light like a flame. Her lips parted slightly as he stared at them. Her breathing grew shallow, her creamy breasts rising and falling more rapidly.

He could see the pulse thrumming in her neck. A very male sort of satisfaction slid through him. Lia was not immune, no matter how she bristled and glared.

Zach reached up and ran his thumb over the pulse at her throat. She gasped, but she didn't pull away.

"We were good together," he purred. "We could be again."

Her eyes were wide as she gazed up at him. "This is an arrangement, Zach," she said, her voice hardly more than a whisper. "An arrangement that does not include sex."

He was beginning to regret that he'd used that word with her. She was intent on keeping it strictly business since he'd told her this was a temporary solution to protect their families from the media.

He'd fully intended it to be temporary when he'd said it. It had seemed the perfect solution. He didn't know the first thing about being a father, wasn't sure he could even do it. If he married Lia, gave their child a name and a legacy, they could go their separate ways in a few months and everything would be fine.

Except, strangely, since the moment the doctor had given him the test results earlier, he'd felt a sense of duty that warred with those thoughts.

And more than duty. When Lia had come downstairs tonight, he'd felt the same shot of lust he'd experienced in his room in Palermo. The same hard knot of desire had coiled inside his gut and refused to let go.

He bent toward her, breathed in her scent. "What is your perfume, Lia?" he asked, his breath against her ear. A shudder rolled through her. He could feel it in his fingertips where they pressed into her back and throat.

"It's my own," she said, her voice husky. "I went to a perfumer in the village. She made it for me."

Zach breathed again. "Vanilla. A hint of lavender. Perhaps even a shot of lemon. For tartness," he finished.

"I—I don't know," she said quickly. "I didn't ask."

Zach couldn't stop himself from what he did next. He touched his tongue to her throat, glided to the sweet spot beneath her ear. The sound that came out of her made him hard.

Her hands were on his lapels, clutching him. "Zach, stop…"

"Do you really want me to?" he said against her sweet flesh.

She shuddered again, and he reacted with animal instinct, pushing her into an alcove where they were hidden from prying eyes. Unless someone was standing right in front of the opening, they would not be visible from down the corridor.

It was appalling behavior for a public event, but right now Zach was operating on a pure shot of desire.

"I definitely taste lemon," he said, tilting her chin up and back until her eyes were on his. "You are so beautiful, Lia. So hot."

"You are trying to seduce me," she said, closing her eyes. "You would say anything to further your purpose."

His hand slid around her back, up her rib cage. He shaped her breast, his thumb caressing her nipple beneath the fabric. He was gratified when it pebbled beneath his touch.

"Why do you say such things? Why don't you want to believe the truth? If you weren't hot, I wouldn't be unable to control myself with you. Don't you remember how it felt? How we burned together?"

"I remember it every day," she said, still not looking at him. "I carry a reminder."

He let his hand fall to her belly, pressed gently against her there. She uttered a little protest, but he didn't take his hand away. He knew it bothered her that her belly wasn't hard and lean. No, she was soft and pliable, womanly. Her body was curvy, not angular and hard from exercise. He liked it just the way it was.

"Maybe we should alter the arrangement," he said, his tongue suddenly feeling thick in his mouth. As if he didn't know the right thing to say. As if he were so new at this game of seducing a woman that the outcome could be in doubt.

She turned her head toward him, as if she was going to speak, and he knew the answer wouldn't be what he wanted to hear from the way she stiffened at his words.

But he wasn't going to give her a chance to say a thing. He brought his mouth down on hers, trapping her body between him and the wall. His heart was thundering in his chest, the way it did when he'd gotten that adrenaline rush after he'd aimed his jet straight up and climbed the sky like it was a mountain. Once he'd stopped climbing and starting racing toward earth again, only to pull up before it was too late, the g-forces holding him tight to his seat, he'd gotten another huge rush that made him laugh out loud at the sheer joy of flight.

Kissing Lia was similar to that feeling. Her lips were soft beneath his, though he sensed she didn't want them to be. Her hands curled into fists on his lapels—but she didn't push him away. He ghosted a thumb over her nipple and she gasped, letting his tongue inside her mouth.

Another shot of unfiltered desire ricocheted into his groin, making him painfully hard. He'd not been with a woman since he'd been with her. And before that, he'd not been with a woman in months. Lia had been the one to break the drought—and, strangely, he still desired her the way a man desired cool water after a hot trek in the desert.

Zach slid his tongue along hers, coaxed her into responding. She made a little noise in her throat—desire, frustration, he didn't know which—but she stroked him in return. He tightened his grip on her, pulled her in closer to his body.

And then he assaulted her mouth more precisely, more urgently, taking everything she had to give him and demanding yet more. Her arms went around his neck, and then her body was arching into his, her hips pressing ever closer to that hardness at the core of him.

He cupped her ass with both hands, pulled her tightly to him, so tightly there could be no doubt what he wanted from her. He flexed his hips, pressing his hardness into her, finding that precise spot that made her gasp and moan.

He could make her come this way. He *would* make her come this way. He needed to hear her pleasure, needed to be the one to make her feel it.

Dimly, the click of heels against tile registered in his brain. The sound was coming closer, closer. With a frustrated groan, Zach broke away from the sweet taste of Lia. She looked up at him, blinking dazedly, her eyes slightly unfocused and distant, her lips moist and shiny. By degrees, her features changed, set, hardened into a cool mask.

"I'm sorry," he said right before the heels clicked to a stop in front of the alcove. Except he didn't know what he was sorry for.

"Mr. Scott?"

Zach closed his eyes for a brief moment. Then he turned to greet the socialite who stood there. "Yes, Mrs. Cunningham?"

Elizabeth Cunningham's gaze darted past him to Lia,

then back again. He didn't miss the tightening of Elizabeth's mouth, or the disapproving gleam in her eye. It pissed him off. Royally. Elizabeth Cunningham was thirty years younger than her husband, and much too judgmental for one who'd reached the pinnacle of society by marrying into it.

Zach reached for Lia's hand, pulled her to his side. Claimed her. He thought she might move away from him, but she didn't. She seemed to grasp the importance of appearances, after all.

"It's time for your speech," the other woman said, her gaze settling on his face once more.

Zach made a show of looking at his watch. "Ah, yes, so it is. I lose track of time when I'm with my lovely fiancée, I'm afraid."

Elizabeth's eyes widened. They darted to Lia. To Lia's credit, she didn't flinch or give away by look or gesture that she was anything other than what he'd said she was.

"Come, darling," he told her, tucking her hand into his arm and leading her back toward the gathered crowd. Another speech, another event to tick off his social calendar.

Afterward, he would take Lia home…and then he'd finish what he'd started here tonight.

Lia was shell-shocked. She sat through the rest of the evening in a daze. Her mouth still tingled where Zach had kissed her. Her body throbbed with tension and need. She'd been so furious with him, so convinced she would never, ever be susceptible to his charms again.

She'd been wrong. Woefully, pitifully wrong.

She was still the same lonely girl she'd always been, the same girl looking for acceptance and affection. She despised herself for that weakness, despised Zach for taking advantage of it. She took a sip of her water and let her gaze slide over the crowd before turning back to Zach.

He stood at a podium close to their table, talking about his father, about the war, about the night he was shot down over enemy territory. He said the words, but she wasn't convinced he felt any of them.

He was detached. Cold. The crowd was not. They sat rapt. And Lia couldn't help herself. She was rapt with them. She learned about how his plane took a hit and he'd had to bail out. How he'd broken his leg in the landing, and how he'd had to drag himself to shelter before the enemy found him.

Then she listened to him talk about the six marines who'd been sent in to extract him after several days. They had all died trying to save him. He was the only survivor. It sent a chill down her spine and raised the hairs on the back of her neck.

He'd suffered much, she thought. So much that she couldn't even begin to understand. She wanted to go to him, wanted to wrap her arms around him and lower his head to her shoulder. And then she just wanted to hold him tight and listen to him breathe.

Toward the end of his speech, a photographer started to take photos. His flash snapped again and again. Zach seemed to stiffen slightly, but he kept talking, kept the crowd in the grip of his oratory. The photographer moved in closer. No one seemed to think anything of it, but Lia remembered that night in Palermo and her palms started to sweat.

Zach gripped the sides of the podium, his knuckles white. The flash went off again and again and she didn't miss the way he flinched in reaction. It was so subtle as to seem a natural tic, but something told Lia it was not. Then he seemed to stumble over his thoughts, repeating something he'd just said. Panic rose up in Lia's chest, gripped her by the throat.

She couldn't watch him lose his way like he had in Palermo. She couldn't let him suffer that kind of public meltdown. She didn't know that he would, but she couldn't get past the memory of the way she'd met him, plastered against that wall with his eyes tight shut and the flashing and booming of lights and bass all around.

She didn't have to look at this crowd any longer to know it would be disastrous if he did.

Right now, everyone seemed to be paying attention to Zach. She didn't quite know what to do, or how to deflect their attention—and then she did. She coughed. Loudly. After a moment, Zach's gaze slid in her direction. She kept coughing, and then she reached for the water, took a swallow as if she were having trouble. Zach's attention was firmly on her now. He darted his eyes over the crowd, but they inevitably came back to her.

She coughed again, sipped more water. The photographer seemed satisfied enough with his photos thus far that he lowered his camera and melted toward the back of the crowd.

Lia stopped coughing. A few minutes later, Zach wound up his speech. The room erupted in applause. Lia breathed deeply, relieved. Though, perhaps Zach had been in control the whole time. Perhaps he'd never needed her intervention, lame though it was.

She watched him walk toward her. People stopped him, talked to him, making his progress back to her side take quite a long time. But then he was there, and she was gazing up at him, searching his face for signs of stress.

There were none.

He gazed over her head, his attention caught by something. Just for a moment, his mouth tightened. The flash went off again and Lia whirled toward the source.

"Come, darling," Zach said, holding out his hand. "Let's get you home."

Several of the Washington elite slid sideways glances at them, but Lia didn't care. She gave Zach a big smile and put her hand in his. He helped her from her chair and then they were moving toward the exit. They were waylaid a few more times, but soon they were on the street and Lia sucked in a relieved breath. They were facing the National Mall and the street was far quieter here since it fronted the museums instead of busy Constitution Avenue.

Raoul pulled up in the Mercedes on cue. Zach didn't wait for him to come around and open the door. He yanked it open and motioned Lia inside. Then he joined her and they were speeding off into the night. Zach leaned back against the seat and closed his eyes. His palms were steepled together in his lap.

She found herself wanting to trace a finger along the hard line of his jaw. She would not do it, of course.

"Are you all right?" she asked presently.

His eyes opened. "Fine. Why?"

She fiddled with the beading on her gown. "I thought the photographer might have disturbed you."

Zach was very still. "Not at all," he said after a moment's hesitation. "It goes with the territory. I am accustomed to it."

His answer disappointed her, but she decided not to push him further. She remembered how angry he'd been in Palermo, how disgusted with himself. She'd hoped he might confide in her tonight, but she had to understand why he did not.

Still, she ached for him.

"I'm sorry those things happened to you," she said. "In the war."

He shrugged. "That's what war is, Lia. Brutal, inhumane. People get hurt and people die. I'm one of the lucky ones."

Lucky ones. He didn't sound as if he believed those words at all. And yet he was lucky. He was here, alive—and she was suddenly very thankful for that. Her chest squeezed tight as she thought of what he'd said tonight—and how very close she'd come to never knowing him at all.

"Why don't you fly anymore, Zach?" She remembered that he'd said he couldn't but she didn't know why. She'd asked him that night in Palermo, but then she'd told him not to answer when she'd thought she'd crossed a line into something too personal.

Now, however, she wanted to know. She felt like she needed to know in order to understand him better. Her heart beat harder as she waited.

He sighed. And then he tapped his temple. "Head trauma. Unpredictable headaches accompanied by vision loss. Definitely not a good idea when flying a fighter jet at thirty thousand feet."

He sounded so nonchalant about it, but she knew how much it must hurt him. "I'm sorry."

His eyes gleamed as he looked at her. "Me, too. I loved flying."

"I don't like to fly," she said. "I find it scary."

He grinned, and it warmed her. "That's because you don't understand how it works. By that, I mean the noises the plane makes, the process of flight—not to mention the fact you aren't in control. It's some unseen person up there, holding your life in his or her hands. But it's all very basic, I assure you."

"I know it's mostly safe," she said. "But you're right. I haven't flown much, and the sounds and bumps and lack of control scare me."

She'd longed for a sedative on the long flight from Sicily, but she hadn't dared take one because of the baby.

His laugh made a little tendril of flame lick through her. "A fighter jet is so much more intense. The engines scream, the thrust is incredible and the only thing keeping you from blacking out is the G suit."

Lia blinked. "What is a G suit?"

"An antigravity suit," he said. "It has sensors that tell it when to inflate. It fits tight around the abdomen and legs in order to prevent the blood draining from the brain during quick acceleration."

Lia shivered. "That sounds frightening."

He shrugged. "Blacking out would be frightening. The suit not so much. You get used to it."

"You miss flying, don't you?"

He nodded. "Every damn day."

"Then I'm sorry you can't do it anymore."

"Me, too." He put his head back on the seat and closed his eyes. She wanted to reach out and touch him, wanted to run her fingers along his jaw and into his hair. But she didn't.

She couldn't breach that barrier, no matter how much she wanted to. She didn't know what she really meant by such a gesture, what she expected. And she couldn't bear it if he turned away from her. If he rejected her.

Lia clasped her hands in her lap and turned to look at the White House as they glided by on Constitution Avenue, heading toward the Lincoln Memorial and the bridge across the Potomac. The monuments were brightly lit, glowing white in the night. Traffic wasn't heavy and they moved swiftly past the sites, across the bridge and toward Zach's house in Virginia.

Lia racked her brain for something to say, something basic and innocuous. No matter what he'd said about the photographer, she was certain he'd had trouble with the intrusiveness of the flash.

But she didn't feel she could push the subject. He'd already shared something with her when he'd told her why he could no longer fly, and how much he missed it. He had not said those things during his speech. He'd said them to her, privately, and she knew it bothered him a great deal.

She was still trying to think of something to say when Zach's phone rang. He opened his eyes and drew it from his pocket, answering only once he'd looked at the display. He spent the next fifteen minutes discussing his schedule with someone, and then the car was sliding between the gates and pulling up in front of the house.

Zach helped her out of the car and they passed inside as a uniformed maid opened the door. It was dark and quiet inside. The maid disappeared once Zach told her they needed nothing else this evening.

The grand staircase loomed before them, subtly lit with wall sconces that went up to the landing. Zach took Lia's elbow and guided her up the stairs. His touch was like a brand, sizzling into her, and her breath shortened as all her attention seemed to focus on that one spot. She didn't want to feel this heat, this curl of excitement and fear that rolled in her belly, but she couldn't seem to help it.

The way he'd touched her earlier, kissed her—

Lia swallowed. She shouldn't want him to do it again, and yet a part of her did. A lonely, traitorous part of her. She wanted him to need her, wanted him to share his loneliness with her.

He escorted her to the room she'd been shown to earlier. But he didn't push her against the wall the way he had in the museum. His hand fell away from her elbow and he took a step back.

Disappointment swirled in her belly, left her feeling hot and achy and empty. After that blazing kiss in the art museum, she'd expected something far different. And after his speech tonight, she'd wanted something far different. That was the Zach she wanted to know—the one who hid his feelings beneath a veneer of coldness, who'd watched six marines die and who would never fly again, though he loved it.

That was the Zach he buried deep, the one he'd let out in Palermo. The one she wanted again.

"You did well tonight," he said. Still so cool, so indif-
ferent.

Lia dropped her gaze as another emotion flared to life inside her. Confusion. Maybe she was wrong. Maybe he was
just very good at being what the situation required. War hero.
Senator's son. Fiery lover. "Thank you."

"Good night, Lia." He leaned forward and kissed her
cheek. The touch was light, almost imperceptible. His hands
were in his pockets.

She blinked up at him. "Good night, Zach."

He didn't make a move to leave so she opened her door
and went inside her room because she thought that was what
he wanted her to do. Then she turned and pressed her ear
against the door, straining to hear him as he walked away.
Her heart pounded in her chest.

What if he didn't go? What if he knocked on her door instead? What if she opened it and he took her in his arms and
said he needed her?

What would she do?

Maybe she should open the door. Just yank it open and
confront him. Ask him why he'd kissed her like that earlier.
Why he'd mentioned altering the arrangement and then acted
like it never happened.

Her fingers tightened on the knob. She would do it. She
would jerk it open. She would demand an answer and she
wouldn't fear rejection—

Footsteps moved away down the hall. A door opened and
closed.

Lia wanted to cry out in frustration. She'd waited too long.

The moment was gone.

CHAPTER EIGHT

IT WAS STILL DARK when Lia woke. She lay in bed, uncertain for the first few moments where she was. And then she remembered. She was in Zach's house, in a guest room. She reached for her phone to check the time—2:00 a.m.

Lia yawned and pressed the button to open her mail. Four new messages popped into her inbox, but only one caught her attention.

From: Rosa Corretti
To: Lia Corretti
Subject: Hi

Lia's pulse thrummed as she clicked on the message. She read through it quickly, and then went back to the beginning to make sure she'd read it right the first time. Rosa was actually writing to her. There wasn't a snarky word or single insult in the entire missive. In fact, there was a word Lia had never expected to see: *Sorry.*

Rosa was sorry for snapping at her after Carmela's outburst. Not only that, but her half sister said she'd been thinking about many things and that she realized how rotten it must have been for Lia to live with Teresa and Salvatore once her father remarried and had a new family.

Rosa wouldn't know that Lia had actually been sent away

long before Benito remarried. Why would she? Until just now, Lia was pretty sure Rosa barely remembered her existence, much less thought about her in any capacity.

Still, it was nice to hear from her. Surprising, but nice.

Lia would answer her, most definitely, but she wasn't about to get her hopes up for what their relationship could be. She'd spent her entire life mostly forgotten, and she wasn't planning to stick her neck out now. She didn't really know Rosa, but she knew what kind of woman Carmela was. Hopefully her daughter was nothing like her, but Lia intended to proceed with caution.

She got out of bed and slipped on her robe. Even thinking about Carmela had the power to make her feel badly about herself. When she remembered the way Zach had left her at her door tonight, the feeling intensified. It had taken her some time, but she'd figured out what he'd been doing at the museum when he'd kissed her.

He'd been getting her under control after she'd broken out of the box he'd put her in for the night. She'd dared to show temper, and he'd managed to smooth it over and make her forget for a while. He'd tugged her into the corner he wanted her in and tied her up neatly with a bow.

She'd sat there like a good girl, smiling and applauding and worrying over him. It infuriated her to remember how compliant she'd been, and all because he'd pressed her against that wall and made her remember what it had been like between them.

Heat crawled up her spine, settled between her legs and in her core. In spite of it all, her body still wanted his. It angered her to be so out of control of her own reactions, to feel so needy around a man who clearly didn't need her.

Lia went to the French doors and pulled them open, hoping the night air would help to cool her down.

A mistake, because it was summer in Virginia and the

night air wasn't precisely cool. Oh, it was far cooler than it had been in the heat of the day, but it was still quite warm.

There was a breeze, however. Lia stepped outside and walked barefooted across the stone terrace to the railing. The strong scent of lavender rose from the pots set along the wall. She ran her fingers over the blooms, brought them to her nose. It made her think of home.

If she could add lemon to the mix, she'd be transported to Sicily. Except that Sicily didn't quite feel like home any longer, she had to admit. Since the moment she'd fallen into Zach's arms at the wedding, she'd felt a restlessness that hadn't gone away. Sicily had seemed too small to contain her, too lonely.

But coming to the States was no better. She was still alone.

She could hear the river gurgling over boulders in the distance. The moon was full, its pale light picking out trees and grass and the foaming water where it rolled over rocks.

It was peaceful. Quiet, other than the river and the sound of a distant—very distant—dog barking. She leaned against the railing and tried to empty her mind of everything but sleep.

It was difficult, considering her body was on another time zone. Not only that, but she also had a lot on her mind. She'd fled Sicily because she'd been scared of what her family would do, but she'd never considered what Zach would do. Or what her life would become once she was with him.

Was it only yesterday that she'd stood in a hotel and told him their arrangement would be in name only? And now here she was, aching for his touch, and simply because he'd kissed her tonight with enough heat to incinerate her will.

She was weak and she despised herself for it. She didn't fit in, not anywhere, and she wanted to. Zach had held out the promise of belonging on that night in Palermo—and she'd leaped on it, not realizing it had been a Pandora's box of endless heartache and trouble.

There was a noise and a crash from somewhere behind her. Lia jumped and spun around to see where it had come from. It seemed to be from farther down the terrace, from another room. Her heart was in her throat as she stood frozen, undecided whether to run into her room and close the door or go see what had happened. What if it were Zach? What if he needed her?

But then a door burst open and a man rushed through and Lia gasped. He was naked, except for a pair of dark boxer shorts. He went over to the railing and leaned on it, gulping in air. He dropped his head in his hands. His skin glistened in the night, as if he'd just gotten out of a sauna.

The moonlight illuminated the shiny round scar tissue of the bullet wound in the man's side. Zach.

As if it could be anyone else. Her heart went out to him.

"Is everything okay?" she asked softly.

He spun toward her, his body alert with tension. Briefly, she wondered if she should run. And then she shook herself. No, she would not run.

Zach wasn't dangerous, no matter that he'd told her he was in Palermo.

"You're okay, Zach," she said, moving cautiously, uncertain if he was still caught in the grips of a dream or an episode like the one in Palermo. "It's me. It's Lia."

He scraped a hand through his hair. "I know who it is," he said, his voice hoarse in the night. The tension in him seemed to subside, though she knew it was still right beneath the surface. "What are you doing outside in the middle of the night?" he demanded.

She ignored his tone. "I could ask the same of you."

He turned toward the railing again, leaned on it. It was such a subtle maneuver, but it warmed her because it meant, on some level, at least, that he trusted her. After what he'd been through in the war, she didn't take that lightly.

"I had a dream," he said. The words were clipped and tired.

Lia stepped closer, until she could have touched him if she reached out. She didn't reach out. "And it was not a good one," she said softly.

He shook his head. Once. Curtly. "No."

"Do you often dream of the war?"

He swung to look at her. "Who said I was dreaming of the war?"

She thought of the wild look in his eyes when he'd first looked at her, at the way he'd seemed to be somewhere else instead of here, and knew she was right. Just like that night in Palermo, though he had been wide awake then.

"Is it the same as what happened when I first met you? Or different?"

He didn't say anything at first. He simply stared at her. The moonlight limned his body, delineating the hard planes and shadows of muscle. She had an overwhelming urge to touch him, but she clenched her hands tightly at her sides instead.

She would not reach for him and have him push her away. She'd done that too many times in her life, when she'd reached out to family and been shunned instead.

"You don't quit, do you?" he asked.

"You can deny it if you like," she said. "But I think we both know the truth."

"Fine." He blew out a breath. "It's different than Palermo. When I dream, it's much worse."

"Do you want to talk about it?"

He laughed suddenly. A broken, rusty sound. "God, no. And you don't want to hear it, Lia. You'd run screaming back to Sicily if you did. But thanks for trying."

Lia bristled at his presumption. "I'm tougher than I look."

He shook his head. "You only think you are. Forget it, kitten."

Kitten. She didn't know whether to be insulted or warmed by that endearment. "The photographer did bother you."

"Yes."

There was a warning in his tone. But she couldn't leave it, not now.

"Why do you do these things if you're worried about your reaction?"

He growled. "Because I have no choice, Lia. I'm a Scott, and Scotts do their duty. And you'd better get used to it because soon you'll be one of us."

It suddenly made her angry. Why should people do things that hurt them just to please other people? "So you're saying I must put myself in situations that cause me stress for the sake of the Scotts?"

His eyes flashed. "Something like that."

She lifted her chin. "And if I refuse?"

"Too late to back out now, babe. I told Elizabeth Cunningham you were my fiancée. Tomorrow, the papers will be filled with you and me. The whole city will be interested in the woman who captured my heart. And you will be at my side for every damn event I have to attend. Like it or not."

A tremor slid through her. "You're no different than my grandfather was," she said bitterly. "It's all about appearances. The family. What will people think? What will they do if they know we're human, too?" Lia cursed in Italian. "We can't have that, can we? Because the family reputation is everything."

So long as you didn't shame the family, so long as you kept your mouth shut and your head down, you could stay. But, oh, don't expect them to care about you.

Don't ever expect that. She put her hand over her belly

and vowed with everything in her that her child would never
for one minute think public façades were more important
than feelings. It was untenable, no matter the importance
of the family.

She started to turn away, but Zach gripped her arms. She
tried to pull out of his hold, but he wouldn't let her go. His
face was so close to hers. And, in spite of her fury, her body
was softening, aching. She hated that he did that to her. Especially when she did no such thing to him in return.

"Some things are bigger than our own desires," he said.
"You know that."

Lia sucked in a breath that shook with tears. "And some
things are more important than appearances." She thought of
him at the podium, of the way he'd looked when he'd started
to fight the demons in his head, and then of the way he'd
rushed out onto the terrace tonight, and she couldn't stand
that he would have to face the same issue again and again,
and all for the sake of his family reputation. "Maybe you
should talk to someone—"

He let her go and shoved back, away from her. Then he
swore. Explosively.

A second later he was back, one long finger inches from
her nose. It trembled as he pointed. If not for that single detail, she would have been frightened of his temper.

"Leave it, Lia. It's none of your business," he growled.
The finger dropped and he spun away, put both hands on
the railing and stood there, drawing in breath after breath
after breath.

She didn't know quite what to say. She hadn't thought her
suggestion would cause him such pain, but clearly it had. She
hated that it did. And she hated that he wouldn't share with
her. That he lost his cool, but wouldn't tell her what she so
desperately wanted to know to help him.

She closed her eyes and swallowed, and then closed the distance between them until she was beside him. He didn't move or speak, and neither did she.

"I'll do my duty, Zach," she said softly. "I'll be at every event you are. And I won't let them get to you."

No matter what she'd said about refusing to go along, she wouldn't leave him to face those situations alone. Not after tonight. He needed someone with him, and she would be that someone.

He turned toward her, his brows drawn down in a question.

She lifted her chin and tumbled onward. She felt silly, but it was too late to turn back.

"The photographers. The flashes. The crowds. Whatever it is, I won't let them derail you or trigger a reaction. You can count on me."

His expression didn't change, but his nostrils flared. "You're offering to protect me?"

Oh, it did sound so ridiculous when he put it like that. On impulse, she reached for his bare arm, squeezed the hard muscle encouragingly while trying to ignore the heat sizzling into her.

"Whatever it takes," she said. And then, because her cheeks were hot with embarrassment and she didn't want to hear what he might say in response, she turned and walked away.

"Lia."

She was to her door when he called out. She turned to face him, her hands at her sides, trying for all the world to seem casual and calm. "Yes?"

"Grazie, cara mia."

Her heart skipped. "You're welcome," she said. And then she stepped into her room and closed the door with a quiet, lonely click.

* * *

The day did not promise to be a good one. Zach turned up the speed on the treadmill, forcing himself to run faster. He needed to reach that Zen moment of almost total exhaustion before he could consider himself in any shape to deal with everything coming his way today.

The sun hadn't yet peeked over the horizon, and the sky was still gray and misty from the river. Soon, however, all hell would break loose.

As if the hell of his dream hadn't been enough to endure. He squared his jaw and hit the speed button. He'd been back in the trench, immobile from the drugs the medic had given him, and listening to the shouts and rat-a-tat-tats of gunfire. The marines had been cool, doing their job, but they'd known air support wasn't coming in time.

He'd wanted to help so badly. He could still see the last marine, still feel the pistol grip in his hand as the man gave him a weapon. He'd lifted it, determined to do what needed to be done—

But he always woke at the moment he pulled the trigger. Terrified. Angry. Disgusted.

Sweat poured down his face, his naked torso. He ran faster, but he knew from experience he couldn't outrun the past.

No, he had to focus on today. On what was coming his way after last night.

First, there would be the papers. Then there would be an angry phone call from his father, Senator Zachariah J. Scott, demanding to know who Lia was and what the hell was going on.

Zach almost relished that confrontation. Except he didn't want Lia hurt. He should have chosen a better way to an-nounce her role in his life, but he'd been too angry to think straight once Elizabeth Cunningham had looked at her like she was another piece of flotsam moving across his orbit. He'd simply reacted. Not the way he'd been trained to deal with things, but too late now.

She would handle it, though. He pictured her last night when he'd cornered her before his speech. She'd been fierce, angry, determined.

Sexy.

God, she was sexy. Something about Lia's special combination of innocence and fierceness was incredibly sexy to him. Addictive.

She wasn't like the women he'd been linked with in the past. They had always been polished, smooth, ready to step in and become the perfect society wife. Oh, he'd had his flings with unsuitable women, too. Women who were wild, fun, completely inappropriate.

Lia fit none of those categories. She wasn't smooth and polished, but she wasn't inappropriate, either. He doubted she was wild, though she'd certainly been eager and willing during their two-night fling.

Zach gritted his teeth and resolved not to think about that. Not right now anyway.

But he couldn't stop thinking about last night on the terrace when she'd said she would protect him. He'd wanted to laugh—but he hadn't. It had been incongruous, her standing there in her silky pajamas, looking all soft and womanly, staring up at him and telling him she would be at his side, making sure he didn't have a meltdown because of a camera flash or a nosy reporter.

He'd been stunned and touched at the same time. Yes, he'd nearly growled at her. He'd nearly told her she was too naive and to mind her own business. But her eyes had been shining up at him and she'd looked so grave that he'd been unable to do it.

He'd realized, looking at her, that she really was serious.

That she cared, on some level, and that if he was nasty to her, she would crumple inside.

So he'd swallowed his anger and his pride and he'd thanked her. It had been the right thing to do, even if the idea of her protecting him was ridiculous.

Except that she had intervened during his speech, coughing when he'd stumbled on the words. At the time, he'd thought little of it, though he'd been grateful to have something to focus on besides the photographer.

Now he wondered if she'd done it on purpose.

Zach finished his workout, showered and dressed, and went into his office to read the papers. The phone call came at seven. He let it ring three times before he picked it up.

"Care to tell me what's going on, Zach?" His father's voice was cool and crisp, like always. They'd never had a close relationship, though it was certainly more strained since Zach had come home from the war.

He knew his father loved him, but feelings were not something you were supposed to let show. They made you weak, a target to those who would exploit them.

And there wasn't a single aspect of his father's life that hadn't been thought out in triplicate and examined from all angles—except for one.

The only thing he hadn't been able to control was falling in love with his wife. It was the one thing that made him human.

"I'm getting married," Zach said, his voice equally as cool.

He heard the rustling of the newspaper. The *Washington Post*, no doubt. "I see that. The question is why."

"Why does anyone get married?"

His father snorted softly. "Many reasons. Love, money, comfort, sex, children. What I want to know is which reason it is for you. And what we need to do on this end."

A thread of anger started to unwind inside him. It was his life they were talking about, and his father was already looking at it like it was something to be handled and packaged for the world to digest. "For the spin, you mean."

"Everything needs to be spun, Zach. You know that."

Yes, he certainly did. From the time he was a child and his father had decided to step away from Scott Pharmaceuticals and put his hat in the political ring, their lives had been one big spin job. He'd grown sick of the spin. He'd thought going into the military and flying planes would be authentic, real, a way to escape the fishbowl of his powerful family's life.

He'd been wrong. It had simply been another chance for spin. Hero. All-American. Perfect life. Doing his duty. Father so proud.

How proud would his father be if he knew Zach hated himself for what had happened out there? That he wished he'd died along with the marines sent to rescue him? That he was no hero?

"But your mother and I love you," his father was saying. "We want to know what's going on in truth."

Zach's jaw felt tight. "She's pregnant," he said, and then felt immediately guilty for saying it. As if he were betraying Lia. As if it were her secret and not his, too.

He could hear the intake of breath on the other end of the phone. No doubt his father was considering how to minimize the embarrassment of his only son making such a foolish mistake.

Except the idea it was a mistake made him angry. How could it be a mistake when there was a small life growing inside Lia now? A life that was one half of him.

"You are certain the baby is yours?"

Zach ground his teeth together. An expected question, one he'd asked, too, and yet it irritated him. "Yes."

His father blew out a breath. "All right, then. We'll do what we need to do to minimize the damage."

"Damage?" Zach asked, his voice silky smooth and hard at the same time.

And yet had he not thought the very same thing? Had he not proposed this arrangement to Lia in order to minimize the damage to their families—most specifically his?

He had, and it infuriated him that he'd thought it for even a moment. What was wrong with him?

"You know what I mean," his father said tightly.

"I do indeed. But Lia is not a commodity or a project to be managed. She's an innocent young woman, she's pregnant with my child and I'm marrying her just as soon as I get the license."

His father was silent for the space of several heartbeats. "Very well," he said softly. "Your mother and I will look forward to meeting her."

It was the same sort of cool statement his father always made when he wasn't pleased but knew that further argument would result in nothing changing. Zach felt uncharacteristically irritated by it. He knew how his father was, and yet he'd thought for the barest of moments that his parent might actually have a conversation about Lia and marriage instead of one based on how Zach's choices would impact the family.

Zach didn't bother to waste time with any further pleasantries. "If that's all, I have things to attend to," he said in clipped tones.

"Of course," his father said. "We'll be in touch."

Zach ended the call and sat at his desk for several minutes. He'd never once had a meaningful conversation with his father. It bothered him. Instead of telling the older man what kind of hell he'd been through in the war, and how it really made him feel to be treated like a returning hero, he smiled and shook hands and did his duty and kept it buried deep inside.

Because that's what a Scott did.

The gardener rolled a wheelbarrow full of something across the lawn outside. Zach watched his progress. The man stopped by a winding bed of roses and began clipping stems, pruning and shaping the bushes. He was whistling.

Two days ago, Zach had been going about his life as always, attending events, making speeches and feeling empty inside. It was the life he knew, the life he expected.

Now, oddly enough, he felt like those bushes, like someone had taken shears to him and begun to shape him into something else. They were cutting out the dead bits, tossing them on the scrap heap and leaving holes.

He felt itchy inside, jumpy. He stood abruptly, to do what he didn't know, but then Lia moved across his vision and he stopped in midmotion. She was strolling down the wide lawn in the early morning sunshine, her long hair streaming down her back, her lush form clad in leggings and a loose top.

He watched her move, watched the grace and beauty of her limbs, and felt a hard knot form in his gut. She went over to the gardener and started to talk. After a moment, the man nodded vigorously and Lia picked up a set of pruning shears. Zach watched in fascination as she began to cut branches and toss them on the pile.

He suddenly wanted to be near her. He wanted to watch her eyes flash and chin lift, and he wanted to tug her into his arms and kiss her until she melted against him the way she had last night in the art gallery.

CHAPTER NINE

"YOU DON'T NEED to do that."

Lia looked up from the rosebush she'd been pruning to find Zach watching her. She hadn't heard him approach. He stood there, so big and dark and handsome that her heart skipped a beat in response.

He was wearing faded jeans and a navy T-shirt, and his hands were shoved in his pockets. He looked...delicious. And somehow weary, too.

Lia frowned. Larry the gardener had moved farther down the row. He was whistling and cutting, whistling and cutting. If he knew Zach had arrived, he didn't show it. Except that he moved even farther away, presumably out of earshot, and she knew he was aware of his boss's presence, after all.

Lia focused on Zach again. "I know that," she said. "I want to."

Zach's gaze dropped. "You don't have any gloves. What if you scratch yourself?"

Lia glanced down at her bare hands holding the pruning shears. "I'm careful. Besides, I'm not in a race."

She thought he might argue with her, but instead he asked, "Did you work in your grandparents' garden?"

She lopped off a spent bloom and set the shears down to carefully extract it from the bush. "Yes. I enjoy growing things. I'm pretty good at it, too."

"I don't doubt that. But you shouldn't be out here. It's hot, and you're pregnant."

As if in response to his reminder about the heat, a trickle of moisture slid between her breasts. "It's hot in Sicily, too. And the doctor said I should get some exercise. It's not good to sit indoors and do nothing."

"I have a gym, and a perfectly good treadmill. You can walk on it."

"I want to be outside, Zach. I want to be in the garden."

He frowned. "All right, fine. But not more than half an hour at a time, and not after nine in the morning or before five at night."

Lia blinked at him. "Why, thank you, your majesty," she said. "How very generous of you."

"Lia." Zach reached for her hand, took it gently in his. Instantly, a rush of sensation flooded her. She would have pulled free—except that she liked the feeling. "I'm not trying to be difficult. But you aren't used to the heat here. It's oppressively muggy in the summer, and it'll get to you before you realize it. Besides, we have a busy schedule and I don't want you to exhaust yourself."

Lia reached for another bloom with her free hand, only this time she was rattled from his touch and she grasped it too low on the stem. A sharp thorn punctured her thumb and she cried out. Zach swore softly and grabbed her hand. Now, he held both her hands between his.

Blood welled in a bright round bubble on the fleshy pad of her thumb.

"It's fine," she said, trying to pull her hand away.

Zach's grip tightened. "You're coming inside and washing it."

Lia sighed. She knew she wasn't going to win this battle. Besides, it was kind of nice that he was concerned. She shook herself mentally. There was no sense reading more into his concern than there was.

"Fine."

She called to Larry, who waved and smiled after she explained why she had to go. Then she followed Zach up to the house. He led her into the kitchen and slid on the taps. When the water was hot, he poured soap in her hand and made her wash.

"It's a rosebush, Zach, not a used hypodermic needle."

"Better safe than sorry," was all he said.

She finished washing, and then frowned while Zach put a dab of antibiotic ointment on her thumb and covered it with a Band-Aid.

When she looked up at him, his dark eyes were intent on her, his brows drawn down as he studied her. Her heart skipped the way it always did. Angrily, she tamped down on the rising tide of want within her.

"Did you eat breakfast yet?"

"I had a cup of tea and some toast," she said a touch breathlessly.

Zach frowned. "That's not good enough," he muttered, turning away from her and grabbing a pan off the hanging rack. "You need protein."

Lia crossed her arms, bemused suddenly. "Are you planning to cook for me?"

He glanced up at her, still scowling. And then he grinned and she had to catch her breath at the transformation of his features. "I can, actually. I had to learn when I entered the service. The air force frowns on hired help in the bachelor officers' quarters."

A man from a rich family who'd grown up with chefs and servants suddenly having to cook for himself? What an adjustment that must have been.

"Allora," she said. "It's a wonder you didn't starve."

He winked. "I'm a quick learner."

He retrieved eggs and cheese from the refrigerator. The housekeeper came in, took one look at the pan and him and shrugged. She retrieved whatever thing she'd come for—Lia didn't pay attention—and was gone again.

Lia didn't actually think she could eat anything else right now, but she was too fascinated to stop him from cracking the eggs and whipping them.

"So why did you join the air force? Couldn't you have learned to fly planes anyway?"

His back was to her. She wasn't sure what was on his face just then, but he stiffened slightly, the fork ceasing to swirl the eggs for half a second before he started again. She berated herself for injecting a note of discord into the conversation when it had seemed to be going so well.

"I wouldn't have been able to fly fighter jets, no. I could have bought one, I suppose. The older ones come up for sale sometimes—but it's not quite the same. Besides, I wanted to serve my country."

"A noble cause."

He shrugged. "Yes." Then he stopped again, his broad shoulders tight. A moment later, he turned to her. His expression was troubled. "No, that's not why I did it," he said softly. "I joined the military because I wanted to get away from life as Zachariah J. Scott IV. I didn't want the career at Scott Pharmaceuticals, the governorship of a state, the senate run and then maybe the presidency. Those are my father's dreams, not mine. I wanted to do something that mattered."

Lia's heart felt as if it had stopped beating. Dear God, he was sharing something with her. Something important. She didn't want to screw it up.

"You seem to have done that," she said. She thought of the medal in her room and knew he'd gotten it for good reasons. But why had he thrown it away?

He sighed, his shoulders relaxing a fraction. "You'd think so, wouldn't you? But here I am, and all that my time in the military did for me was set me up for even greater success if I were to follow the path my father wants."

"I think those things matter, too, Zach. It takes a lot of sacrifice to serve your country in any manner, don't you think?"

He glanced at her. "You're right, of course. Still…"

"It's not the path you want to take," she said when he didn't finish the sentence.

He slid the pan onto the stove and added a pat of butter. Then he turned on the burner. "No, I don't."

"What do you want, then?"

He looked at her for a long minute. "I want to fly. But I don't get to do that anymore, no matter that I want to." The butter started to sizzle. Zach poured in the eggs and swirled them in the pan.

"Surely there's something else," she said softly.

His gaze was sharp. "I want to help people returning from the war. It's not easy to go back to your life after you've been through hell."

Lia swallowed. He was talking from experience. And it suddenly made something clear. "Which is why you speak at these fundraisers."

"Yeah."

Yet he wasn't comfortable doing it. That much she knew from watching the effect on him last night. Oh, he was good at it—but it took a toll on him each and every time. "That's a good thing, then. I'm sure it makes a difference."

He shrugged. "It helps fund programs to return vets to a normal life. It also keeps the public aware of the need."

The eggs set in the pan, and Zach added the cheese. Soon, he was sliding the omelet onto a plate and carrying it to the kitchen island. He turned to look at her expectantly.

"Coming?"

How could she say no? She was ridiculously touched that he'd made her an omelet, and ridiculously touched that he'd shared something private with her. She walked over to the island and hopped onto the bar stool. Zach retrieved a fork and napkin, poured her a glass of juice and sat across from her, chin on his hand as he watched her take the first bite.

The omelet was good, creamy and buttery, with just the right amount of cheese. But it was hard to eat it when he was watching her. She could feel her face growing hot as she slid a bite between her lips.

"You have to stop staring at me," she finally said when her heart was thrumming and her face was so hot that he surely must see the pink suffusing her skin.

"I want to make sure you eat it all."

"I won't be able to if you don't stop watching me."

He sighed. "Fine." He sat back on the bar stool and turned to look out the window. "Better?"

"Yes. *Grazie*."

Though she hadn't thought she was hungry, the omelet was good enough that she took another bite. Lia glanced up at Zach, and her heart pinched in that funny way it did whenever she realized how very attractive he was. And how little she really knew him.

"Thank you," she said after a minute. "It's very good."

"Hard to mess up an omelet," he said. "But I'm glad you like it."

"I could," she said. "Mess up an omelet, that is."

He turned to look at her. "You can't cook?"

She shrugged. "Not really, no. Nonna tried to teach me, but I'm hopeless with the whole thing. I get the pan too hot or not hot enough. I either burn things or make gelatinous messes. I decided it was best to step away from the kitchen and let others do the work. Better for all involved."

"How long have you lived with your grandparents?"

"Since I was a baby," she said, her heart aching for a different reason now. The old feelings of shame and inadequacy and confusion suffused her. "My mother died when I was little and my father sent me to my grandparents. I grew up there."

"I'm sorry," he said. "I don't know what it's like to lose a mother, but I can't imagine it was easy."

Lia shrugged. "I don't remember her, but I know she was very beautiful. A movie star who fell in love with a handsome Sicilian and gave up everything to be with him. Unfortunately, it didn't work out." She moved a slice of omelet around on the plate. "My father remarried soon after she died."

She could see him trying to work it out. Why she hadn't gone to live with her father and his new wife. Why they'd left a baby with her grandparents. Bitterness flooded her then. She'd often wondered the same thing herself, until she was old enough to know why they didn't take her back. She was simply unwanted.

The words poured out before she could stop them. "My father pretended like his new family was the only family he had. He did not want me. He never sent presents or called or acknowledged me the few times he did see me. It was as if I was someone else's child rather than his."

Zach reached for her hand, enclosed it in his big, warm one. "Lia, I'm sorry that happened to you."

She sniffed. "Yes, well. Now you know why I had to tell you about the baby. I didn't have a father. I wanted one."

"Yeah," he said softly, "I understand."

Ridiculously, a tear spilled down her cheek. She turned her head, hoping he wouldn't see. But of course he did. He put a finger under her chin and turned her back again. She kept her eyes downcast, hoping that if she didn't look at him, she wouldn't keep crying. She didn't want to seem weak or emotional, and yet that's exactly how she felt at the moment.

Thinking of her childhood, and the way her father had rejected her, always made her feel vulnerable. Another tear fell, and then another.

Zach wiped them away silently. She was grateful he didn't say anything else. He just let her cry.

"I'm sorry," she said after a minute. "I don't know why..." Her voice trailed off into nothing as she swallowed hard to keep the knot in her throat from breaking free.

Zach let her go and scraped back from the island. Another moment and he was by her side, pulling her into the warm solidness of his body.

She pressed her face against his chest and closed her eyes. Her arms, she vaguely realized, were around his waist, holding tight. He put a hand in her hair, cupping her head. The other rubbed her back.

"It's okay, Lia. Sometimes you have to let it out."

She held him hard for a long time—and then she pushed away, not because she didn't enjoy being in his arms, but because she was enjoying it too much. Her life was confusing enough already.

"I haven't cried over this in years," she said, not looking at him. "I'm sure it's the hormones."

"No doubt."

She swiped her palms beneath her cheeks and wiped them on her leggings. *Dio*, how attractive she must be right now, with puffy eyes and a red nose.

"It won't happen again," she said fiercely. "I'm over it."

He lifted an eyebrow. "I wonder—do we ever get over the things that affect us so profoundly? Or do we just think we do?"

Lia sniffled. "I'd like to think so. Not that the past doesn't inform our experience, but if all we do is dwell on it, how will we ever have much of a present?"

She felt a little like a hypocrite, considering how often

she'd felt unwanted and out of sync with her family. But she didn't let it rule her. Or she was determined not to. Perhaps that was a better way of saying it. It crept in from time to time, like now, but that didn't mean it was in charge.

His eyes glittered in the morning light. "Precisely. And yet sometimes we can't help but dwell on a thing."

She knew what he meant. "Your dreams."

"That's part of it."

Lia closed her eyes for a moment. She was in over her head with this. How could what she'd been through compare to his ordeal? Shot down, injured, nearly killed, watching others be killed before your eyes. It made her shiver.

"I think maybe there's something in our psyches that won't let go," she said. "Until one day it does."

He looked troubled. "There were things that happened out there, things—"

He stopped talking abruptly, turned his head to look out the window. His jaw was hard, tight. But he swallowed once, heavily, and her heart went out to him.

"What things?" she whispered, her throat aching. When he turned back to her, his eyes were hot, burning with an emotion that stunned her. Self-loathing? It didn't seem possible, and yet...

He opened his mouth. And then closed it again. Finally, he spoke. "No," he said, shaking his head. "No."

Jesus, he was losing his mind. She'd been here for two days and he wanted to tell her everything. He wanted to take her to his bed, strip her naked and worship every last inch of her body. Which she would not allow him to do if he told her his darkest fears. His deepest secrets.

If she knew how flawed he was, she'd run far and fast in the opposite direction. She'd take that baby in her womb and get the hell away from him. Hell, she'd probably get a restraining order against him.

Her eyes were wide and blue as she sat on that bar stool and looked up at him. Innocent.

God, Lia was so very innocent. She would never understand what he'd been through, or what he'd almost done out there in that trench. Hell, he didn't understand it himself. He lived with the guilt every minute of his life and he still didn't understand it.

She was at a loss for words. He could see that. She dropped her gaze again, and he stepped away from her, breathed in air that wasn't scented with her intoxicating lavender and vanilla and lemon scent.

His body was hard. Aching. He hadn't needed a woman this much in…well, he couldn't remember. The last time had been with her. He wanted her again.

Now wouldn't be soon enough. But she was sweet and delicate and pregnant. She did not need him making sexual demands of her just yet.

Zach rubbed a hand over his head. He couldn't think straight. His entire plan had been to protect his family from scandal—but really, was that the reason? His father had been in office for over two decades now. Would the news his son had knocked up a girl really shock anyone enough that they might not vote for him if he ran for president?

But what if Zach knocked her up and abandoned her to raise the child alone? Yeah, that might raise some heads. But so what?

It was his life, not his father's. Besides, his father had people who spun these things for him. Any scandal of Zach's, unless it involved criminal activities, wasn't likely to touch his father's career—or the funding for the veterans' causes that Zach worked so hard to obtain.

His plan, such as it was, had little to do with protecting anyone, if he were truthful.

And everything to do with the odd pull Lia Corretti had on him.

He wanted her, even if his brain had had trouble figuring that out at first. He'd nearly sent her away. He could hardly credit it at this moment.

"I'm sorry," she finally said. "I shouldn't have asked."

His gaze slewed her way. She was toying with the remains of her omelet. He had a sudden, overwhelming urge to tell her what she wanted to know.

But he couldn't. How could he say the words? He'd never said them to anyone. And if he did, what would she think of him? Would she look at him with terror or pity in her expression?

He couldn't bear either.

"It's not you," he said, because he didn't want to see that hurt expression on her face. She had so much to be hurt about, he realized, now that he knew about her father and what he'd done to her.

Rotten bastard. If the man was still alive, Zach would love to get his hands on him.

He blew out a harsh breath. "It's just…I don't talk about what happened out there. Not to anyone."

"It's okay. I understand."

She wasn't looking at him. He walked over and tilted her chin up with a finger. Her eyes were liquid blue, so deep he could drown in them.

"Do you?" he asked.

"Yes." Her voice was firm. "I know what it's like to have things that hurt you. Things you can't talk about."

The idea anyone had ever hurt her made him want to howl.

She reached up and wrapped her hand around his wrist. It was a soft touch, gentle—and he felt the ricochet effect all the way down to his toes. If he kissed her now, here, would she kiss him back?

"But if you ever want to talk about it," she was saying, "I'm here."

Here. His. He lowered his mouth, brushed his lips gently across hers. Her intake of breath made a current of hot possession slide into his veins. He wanted to hold her closer, kiss her harder.

Instead, he lifted his head and walked away.

CHAPTER TEN

LIA CAREFULLY BRUSHED her hair and donned the dress she'd chosen for this afternoon's cocktail party. Her reflection in the mirror looked the same as always, but she felt as if she'd been changed somehow. Her lips tingled at the thought of Zach, at that light brush of a kiss that had not really been a kiss.

She'd wanted more. She'd wanted to reach up and pull him to her and not let him go until he'd thoroughly kissed her.

And then some.

But he'd walked away without a word. He'd had no trouble doing so. He'd left her sitting there with a half-eaten omelet and a fire inside her that wouldn't go away.

She was mortified. And angry. He might not want her, but he had no right making her want him. If he tried that again, she was going to sock him.

Because her heart couldn't take it. He smiled and laughed and fixed her an omelet, and she wanted to sigh and melt and bask in his presence.

Pitiful, Lia. Just like Carmela had accused her of being. She'd spent so many years wanting to belong to a family that shunned her, and now she was up to her same old tricks with Zach. When would she ever learn? She had her baby now, and that would have to be enough. This thing with Zach was temporary.

He'd told her as much in her hotel room, hadn't he?

Except, dear heaven, when she thought of him this morning, telling her why he'd joined the military and why he continued to book public appearances even though they were difficult for him—well, she wanted to know him. Really know him.

She didn't want this to be temporary when he said things like that. She wanted this to be real. She wanted a chance. They'd gone about it backward, no doubt, but there was something about Zach that hadn't let her have a moment's peace since the instant she'd seen him in that ballroom in Palermo.

She wanted him in her life, and she wanted him to want her.

Lia picked up her perfume and dabbed a very little behind her ears and in the hollow over her collarbone. Then she grabbed her phone to check her email one last time before slipping it into her bag.

There was another email from Rosa. She opened it and read carefully, her heart rising a bit with every line. She had, after careful deliberation, answered Rosa's initial email. Now she had a reply. One that was friendly and open and even a little curious.

Lia sighed. Just when she'd given up on ever having a relationship with any Corretti other than her grandmother, this happened. She was pleased, but she was also baffled. It was as if so long as she wanted a connection, it would always elude her. The moment she stopped caring, or stopped wanting what she wasn't going to get, it happened.

If she could force herself not to care about Zach, would he suddenly be interested?

Lia frowned. If only it worked that way. She dropped her phone into her bag and went to meet Zach. He was waiting for her in the grand living room that overlooked the lawn and the river beyond. He looked up as she walked in, his dark eyes sparking with a sudden heat that threatened to leave her breathless.

His gaze drifted over her appreciatively. Tiny flames of hunger licked at her skin wherever he looked. Then he met her eyes again. The fire in her belly spiked. For a moment, she thought he might close the distance between them and draw her into his arms.

He did not, of course. Zach was nothing if not supremely controlled. Disappointment swirled inside her as they drove to the Lattimores' cocktail party. She kept her gaze focused straight ahead, but she was very aware of Zach's big hand on the gearshift so near her knee.

It was insane to be this crazy aware of a man, and yet she couldn't help it. Zach filled her senses. The more she worked to keep it from happening, the worse it got. He was the sun at the center of her orbit when he was near, no matter how she tried to ignore him.

The event was in a gorgeous mansion in Georgetown. After leaving the car with the valet, Zach escorted her into the gathering, his hand firmly on the small of her back. Lia's stomach vibrated with butterflies. Last night, she'd simply been the woman on his arm at an event. Tonight, she was his fiancée, and the media would take a more pointed interest in her now.

She'd seen the papers in his office, and read the stories about all-American hero Zach Scott and the mystery woman he was suddenly engaged to marry. Of course there was speculation as to why. That didn't surprise her at all.

The story basically went that Zach had traveled to Palermo for a wedding, met the groom's cousin and had a whirlwind romance. They also speculated that she and Zach had conducted this affair over the phone and through email until they simply couldn't stand to be separated any longer.

It was a lovely hypothesis, though laughably far from the truth.

Zach, however, seemed determined to play his role to the hilt once they entered the party. He was the besotted fiancé. He stayed by her side, fetched her drinks, kept a hand on her arm or her waist or her shoulder. Lia took a sip of her non-alcoholic cocktail and tried to calm the racing of her heart.

Zach's touch was driving her insane.

She could hardly remember half the people she met, or half the conversations she had. Her entire focus was on Zach's hand, on his warm, large presence beside her. On the butterflies that hadn't abated. Oh, no, they kept swirling, higher and faster, each time Zach touched her.

It was all she could do not to climb up his frame in front of everyone and kiss him senseless.

Her senses were on red alert, and her body was primed for him. Only him.

It irritated her, but she couldn't stop it. She watched him as he spoke with a gray-haired woman, watched the curve of his mouth when he laughed, the sparkle in his eyes and the long, lean fingers of his hand—the one she could see—as he held his drink.

Lia closed her eyes, tried to blot out the visual of that hand tracing a sensual path over her body. It didn't work, especially since she knew precisely how it would feel.

His arm went around her and she shuddered. "Darling, are you all right?"

Lia looked up at him, into those dark beautiful eyes that seemed full of concern for her. It was an act, she told herself. An act.

Her heart didn't care. It turned over inside her chest—and then it cracked wide-open, filling with feelings she didn't want.

"I—" She swallowed and licked her suddenly dry lips. "I need to freshen up," she blurted.

Without waiting for his reply, she turned and made her way blindly through the crowd until she found an exit. It didn't take her down a hall toward the restrooms, as she'd hoped, but spilled out onto a covered patio that gave way to a manicured garden with a tall hedge. Lia walked right down the path and between the hedges before she realized it was actually a maze.

Her heart beat hard as she breathed in the clean air, hoping to calm down before she went back inside and faced all those people—and Zach—again.

What was the matter with her? Why had she come unglued like that?

Because she was Lia Corretti, that's why. Lost little girl looking for love, for a home, for someone who needed her. She'd been staring at Zach, letting her mind wander, letting her fantasies get the best of her.

And she'd realized, boom, that she felt far more than she should be feeling. That she'd let herself fantasize him right into her heart.

How could you love someone you hardly knew? How could your heart make such a catastrophic mistake?

She hadn't seen it coming. How could she? Of course, she'd thought about him for the past month, thought about their blissful nights together and the way everything between them felt so right—but that was lust, not love.

When did love enter the equation?

When he'd made her an omelet and told her he wanted to do something meaningful with his life? Or earlier, when he'd pulled her against his hard body in Palermo and told her she was beautiful?

"Lia."

She turned at the sound of his voice, her heart thrumming,

her skin flushing hot. She didn't want him here, and yet she did. He moved toward her, so tall, dark and gorgeous that he made her want to weep inside.

How had she let this happen? Panic flooded her as he approached.

But then she had a thought. Maybe—just maybe—it wasn't love, after all. Maybe it was simply a deep infatuation. Yes, she could certainly be infatuated with him. That was far less pitiful than falling in love with a man who was only marrying you because you were pregnant.

Zach came closer, his brows drawn together. "Is everything all right?"

"I needed space," she said. "The crowd was too much."

It wasn't entirely untrue. She wasn't accustomed to so many people. Her life in Sicily had rarely involved crowds or massive gatherings. Her grandparents entertained, and quite frequently, but she hadn't been expected to attend. Now she'd been to three events in as many days, and it was tiring.

"Do you feel well? Should we sit down somewhere?"

"I'm fine," she said quickly.

"Lia." He stopped in front of her, so close she could feel his heat. Her head tilted back to stare up at him. Her breath shortened in her chest as their eyes caught and held. His hands came up to settle on her shoulders, and she felt a deep throbbing note roll through her at that simple touch. "Don't lie to me, *cara mia.*"

She loved it when he spoke to her in Italian.

"Fine, I will tell you," she said. "I feel overwhelmed, Zach. I feel as if I don't really know you, and I won't know you so long as we are constantly putting on a public face. I miss the man I spent time with in Palermo, the one who didn't say or do anything he didn't mean. There were no masks there, no appearances to maintain."

She dropped her gaze, focused on the buttons of his deep

blue shirt. He'd worn a gray pinstripe suit, no tie, and Italian loafers. His jacket was open, and his shirt molded to the hard muscles of his chest. It was custom fit, of course—and the effect was mind-blowing on her already addled brain. He was perfect, beautiful.

For the life of her, she still didn't know what he'd ever seen in her. Or what he ever would see.

"This is my life," he said. "The way it really is. Palermo was an anomaly."

"Yes, well, I choose not to believe that is entirely true. You were more you because you weren't worried about being Zach Scott. You were freer there. You know it's true."

His head dropped for a second. And then he was looking at her again, his gaze dark and mysterious. "Yes."

"That's it? Just yes?"

He sighed. His hands on her shoulders were burning a hole in her. He slid them back and forth, back and forth, and the tension in her body bent like a bowstring. When he slid them to her upper arms, it wasn't a relief.

"You're right. What more do you want me to say?"

She couldn't believe he'd admitted it. But it made something inside her soar that he had. "About which part?"

"That I felt freer in Sicily. I wasn't the main attraction, and I knew it. The press might hound me here, they might follow me if I make a well-publicized trip abroad, but Sicily was unexpected. And too quick to matter much, though of course, they now wish they'd pursued me."

"Why?"

He laughed softly. "Because of you, Lia. Because the confirmed bachelor went to Sicily and came back with a fiancée."

"Thank heavens they didn't," she said, imagining a photographer lurking outside the Corretti Hotel. Or, worse, somehow learning they'd spent two nights together and contriving to get a photo through the open window. Lia shuddered.

"If they had, I doubt any of this would have happened," he said, and her heart twisted in pain. She knew what he meant.

"Perhaps you wish that had been the case." She lifted her chin, trying to hide the hurt she felt deep inside. He was so close. Too close. All she could smell was his delicious scent—a hint of spice and hard masculinity. She wanted to step in, close the distance between them and wrap her arms around him.

Her body ached with the need to feel him inside her again. To be needed by him.

Dio, she was pathetic.

She expected him to agree, to step away, put distance between them and tug her toward the house and the party.

He did not do any such thing. Instead, he slid one of those electric hands up to her jaw, cupped her cheek. The other went to the small of her back, brought her that short step closer, until her body was pressed to his, until she could feel the heat and hardness of him emanating through the fabric of his clothes.

"I should wish it," he said. "But I don't."

Her head was tilted back, her eyes searching the hot depths of his. "I don't know what that means, Zach."

His gaze dropped to her mouth, lingered. And then his lips spread in the kind of wicked smile that made her heart flutter. "I think I'm about to show you, *bella mia*...."

His mouth claimed hers in a hot, possessive kiss that stole her breath and her sense. Lia threaded her arms around his neck without hesitation, melded her body to his. She could do nothing else. She simply wasn't programmed to respond any other way.

The answering hardness in his groin sent a fresh blast of desire ricocheting through her. Had it been this incendiary between them the first time? Had she felt this sweet, sweet fire raging in her belly, her brain, her core? His tongue against hers was nirvana. She couldn't get enough. She kissed him back hotly, desperately, her tongue tangling with his again and again.

He groaned low in his throat, pulling her closer, one hand splayed over her hip, the other sifting into her hair, cupping her head, holding her mouth against his.

She was being swept away on a tide of heat and deep burning feelings that ached to get out. If he kept kissing her like this, she wouldn't survive it. She would not be the same Lia Corretti when it was over.

She would be his creature, his to do with as he wanted. His slave. His, his, his…

With a cry, she pushed him away. She didn't know why, except she knew it was necessary to her sanity, her survival. She could not be any less in control of herself and her emotions than she already was. She could not allow him to own her like this when he gave her nothing of himself in return.

Because she was certain, as certain as she was breathing, that she had no claim on his heart or his emotions. It was physical, this need, nothing more.

For him anyway.

And that was a kind of servitude she did not need. She knew what it was like to be unnecessary—and she could not bear to be so in his life.

He let her go, his hands dropping to his sides. He looked angry, desperate—and then he looked cool, unperturbed. He wiped a thumb across his mouth, across that gorgeous mouth that had been pressed so hotly to hers only moments ago. Then he straightened his shirt, and she was mortified to see that she'd pushed it askew in her desire to touch him.

"Forgive me," he said coolly. "I forgot myself."

Her heart beat hard and swift, and nausea danced in her

stomach. She took a step back, collided with the hedge. Tears filled her eyes, threatening to spill free. What was wrong with her? Why was she so emotional?

"I want to go home," she said.

His head came up, his eyes glittering hard as diamonds. "Home?"

She was confused at his reaction, at the tightness in his voice. "Yes, back to my room. I have a headache, and I want to sleep...."

She wasn't quite certain, but she thought his stance softened, as if a current of tension had drained away. He seemed remote, a gorgeous automaton of a man who stared back at her with cool eyes. He stepped to the side and swept a hand toward the entrance to the maze, indicating that she should precede him.

"Then we'll go," he told her.

They returned to the house in silence. Once there, they played the game again. Lia smiled, though it shook at the corners, as they moved through the gathering. Their leave taking was tedious, but then they were outside and the valet was bringing the car around. There were people clustered together on the mansion's grand portico, waiting for their cars or simply finding another place to take the party.

The lawn was wide, sweeping and, though the property was gated, the gates were opened to the street as cars came and went. A valet pulled up in Zach's BMW while another opened the passenger door for Lia with a flourish. Zach stood by her side. Ordinarily, he would hand her into the car, but this time he didn't touch her. She reckoned he was angry with her.

She took a step toward the car when something bright flashed in her face. It took her a moment to realize they'd been photographed. At first she thought it was simply someone taking a picture they'd ended up in by accident, but when she glanced at Zach, his taut expression told her it was more than that.

He stood there a moment, fists clenched at his side, but then he started around the car when nothing else happened.

The moment he was gone, the photographer took the opportunity to approach again, this time focusing in on Lia. Zach was halfway around the car when he turned to swing back toward the photographer, his face twisted in rage. The valet tried to put himself between Lia and the other man, but the man bumped against him and the car door swung into Lia, knocking her off balance. Before she could save herself, she landed on her hands and knees on the pavement.

Zach was at her side in a second, helping her up, his face tight with fury as he pulled her into the protective embrace of his body. He held her as if he were shielding her from another onslaught. She clung to him, breathed him in, though she told herself she should push away and tell him she was perfectly fine. Her body was still so attuned to his touch that her nerve endings tingled and sparked like fireworks on a summer night.

"Madame, I am so sorry," the valet said. "I tried to stop him—"

"It's not your fault," Zach said, cutting him off abruptly.

"Is the photographer still there?" Lia asked.

"He's gone." Zach pushed her back. "Are you okay?"

Lia nodded. "I think so. My palms hurt, but…"

Zach took her hands and turned them over, revealing scrapes on the heels of her palms. His expression grew thunderous.

"If I ever get ahold of that bastard—"

"I'm fine," Lia said quickly. "It was an accident."

"Your knees," Zach growled, and Lia glanced down. Her knees were scraped and bloody. A trickle of bright red blood ran down the front of her leg.

"I'll be fine," she said. "But I need to wash up."

Zach didn't look convinced. "Maybe we should have a doctor look at you. What if something happened to the baby?"

Lia smiled to reassure him. The scrapes stung, but they weren't life-threatening. She'd had worse the time she got stung by a nest of bees while working in the garden. That could have been life threatening, had she not ran and dived into the pool. "Zach, honestly. I fell on my hands and knees. If babies were hurt by such minor accidents, no one would ever be born."

He frowned, but he ushered her back inside. Their host and hostess were mortified, of course, and they were shown to a private sitting room with an attached bath where Lia could clean up before they went home.

The photographer had disappeared as quickly as he'd arrived. No one could seem to find him. Zach paced and growled like a wounded lion while she sat in the bathroom with a warm wet towel and cleaned the bloody scrapes. He would have done it for her, but she'd pushed him out of the room and told him she could take care of herself.

Once she cleaned the scrapes and stopped the bleeding on her knees, she reemerged to find Zach prowling, his phone stuck to his ear. He stopped when he saw her. He ended the call and pocketed the phone before coming over to her. He looked angry and worried at once.

"I think we should get you to a doctor to be sure," he said.

"Zach, I fell on my hands and knees. I didn't fall off a roof."

He looked doubtful. "I think I'd feel better if someone examined you."

Lia sighed. "Then make an appointment for tomorrow. Tonight, I want to soak in a hot bath and go to bed."

He raked a hand through his hair. "Fine," he said, blowing out a frustrated breath.

This time when they went out to the car, there was no photographer lurking nearby. The gates to the property were closed, opening only when Zach rolled to a stop before them and waited for them to swing open.

It was still light out, because it was summer, but the sun threw long shadows across the road. Zach didn't say anything as they drove, and Lia turned to look at the trees and rocks as they glided down a wide parkway that could have been in the middle of nowhere rather than in a major city.

"We're leaving," Zach said into the silence, and Lia swung to look at him.

"I beg your pardon?"

He glanced at her. "We're not staying here and enduring a media frenzy. I won't have you hurt or scared."

Lia frowned. "Zach, I'm not six years old. I'm not scared, and the hurt is minor. It's annoying, and I'm angry, but I won't break."

"I should have realized this would happen. I should have taken you somewhere else and married you first, then brought you back once they'd had time to get used to it."

Lia didn't know how that would help, considering he was still a Scott and still a media target no matter where he went. "It was an accident. Celebrities get photographed every day, and rarely do any of them fall down when it happens."

Not that she was a celebrity. In fact, that was the problem. She wasn't accustomed to the attention and she hadn't reacted quicker. She'd been surprised, and she'd let her surprise catch her off guard when the valet had tried to help.

"Vegas," Zach said, ignoring her completely. "We'll marry in Vegas, and then we'll go to my house on Maui. They won't be able to get close to us there."

CHAPTER ELEVEN

ZACH DIDN'T KNOW what he was doing. It was a difficult thought to grow accustomed to. He was always sure of his choices, always in charge of his actions. Even when he didn't want to do a thing, like stand in front of a crowd and make a patriotic speech about his time in the service, he did it. And he did it because he'd made a choice. There was an end goal.

Always.

What was his end goal now?

He ran a hand over his face and tried to focus on the computer in front of him. Less than twenty-four hours ago, he'd been at the Lattimores' cocktail party, mingling and schmoozing the guests for contributions to his causes.

Now he was on a jet to Hawaii, having taken a side trip to Las Vegas where he'd stood in a seedy little chapel and pledged to love, honor and cherish Lia Corretti until death do them part.

Which, of course, was a lie.

They would not be together until death.

There was a purpose for this match, a reason they had to join forces. He was protecting her from her family's wrath, first of all. Second, he was avoiding a media scandal that would be troublesome and inconvenient were it to erupt.

Except those reasons no longer felt like the whole truth.

Zach closed the computer with a snap. He couldn't concentrate on business right now. All he could think about was Lia, asleep in the bedroom, her body curled sweetly beneath the sheets, her hair spread out in an auburn curtain he wanted to slide his fingers into.

This need for her was like a quiet, swelling tide. The more he denied it, the stronger and more insistent it grew.

And now he was taking her to a remote location, where the distractions would be minimal. How would he keep his hands off her?

Did he even need to? She'd certainly kissed him back yesterday in the garden. Until that moment when she'd pushed him away, she'd been as into the kiss as he had. He'd forgotten where they were, why he couldn't have her the way he wanted then and there. He'd been ready to lift her skirt and push her back on the grass if it gave him the release he needed.

But she'd been the one to say no. The one to remind him this wasn't normal between them.

Zach snorted. Hell, what was normal anymore? He'd left normal in the rearview the moment his plane disintegrated beneath him and he'd hit the eject button. Nothing since had been the same.

But, for a few minutes yesterday, he'd felt like it had. And, he had to admit, for those blissful few hours in Palermo, too. When he'd been with Lia, he hadn't forgotten—but he'd felt as if he could accept what had happened, what his life had become, and move on.

Why did she do that to him? Why did she make him hope for more?

Lia Corretti—Lia Scott—was a dangerous woman. Dangerous for him. It had taken time, but he'd learned how to live with himself in the aftermath of his rescue.

She threatened to explode it all in his face. To force him

to face the things he kept buried. If he told her, would she understand? Or would she recoil in horror?

He got to his feet and paced the length of the main cabin. A flight attendant appeared as if by magic.

"Did you need anything, sir?"

"Thanks, but no," he said, waving her off again. She disappeared into the galley and he was alone once more.

He was restless, prowling, his mind racing through the facts, through the possibilities. Since he'd met Lia, nothing had been the same. And now they were married, and he was feeling shell-shocked—and hungry.

Hungry for her. He'd thought he could keep it at bay, that this arrangement between them would be tidy. But he'd been wrong. So very wrong.

Soon, he had to do something about this hunger—or go mad denying it.

Maui was bright and beautiful, with a rolling blue surf— which changed from deep sapphire to the purest lapis, depending on the depth—impossibly blue sky and green palm trees that stood in tall clusters, their lush foliage fanning out from the top like a funky hairdo.

Except there were other kinds of palm trees, too, Lia noticed, palms that were short and looked like giant pineapples jutting out of the ground. The tropical flowers were colorful, exotic and so sweetly scented that she fell in love with the island's perfumed air immediately.

A car was waiting at the airport when their private jet landed, and a dark-haired woman in a brightly patterned dress greeted them with leis. Lia's was made of fragrant tuberose and plumeria, while Zach's was open on the end and made from kukui nuts and green ti leaves and tiny puka shells.

They got into the back of a Hummer limo and drove across

an island that was flat in the middle and ringed by mountains. On one side was Haleakala, the tall volcanic mountain that could boast more than one climate. At the bottom, the weather was warm and tropical, but at the top, Zach informed her, it was often windy, rainy and cloudy. It was also bare and cratered, like the surface of the moon. But, before you got that high, there was an Alpine region, with chalets and misty cool air.

It was the oddest thought when all she could see were tall jagged peaks, fields of sugarcane and ocean.

Soon, however, they were on the coast again and driving up a road that led to a stretch of beach dotted with sprawling homes. Eventually, they arrived at one and were met by a man who came and got their bags and took them into the house. Zach lead her into the house and over to the stunning floor-to-ceiling windows that were actually sliding-glass doors. Once the doors were completely open, the house gave way to a sweeping lanai, which was tiered so that part of it sat in the infinity pool. Beyond was the beach, so white and sugary and inviting.

Lia could only stare at how beautiful it was. She came from an island, but one that was completely different from this island. They were both stunning, but Maui was a new experience.

"It's gorgeous," she said when Zach came up beside her again and stood there in silence.

She glanced up at him, and her heart flipped. They were married. *Dio*, she had a husband. She could hardly credit it. Even though he'd told her only a few days ago they would marry, she'd never quite gotten accustomed to the idea it would really happen. She'd been waiting, she could admit now, for that moment when he would decide he didn't want her, after all. When he would send her back to Sicily and the wrath of the Correttis.

Her family might be angry with her when they learned the truth, but at least they would be satisfied she'd gotten married and wouldn't be bringing scandalous shame onto the family by having a baby without a husband.

She wondered if Alessandro knew about the marriage by now. She'd sent a quick email to Rosa when they'd left Las Vegas, and then she'd sent another one to her grandmother. Nonna wasn't online for endless hours, like so many people, but she was technologically proficient and would get the missive soon enough. And she would surely tell the head of the family the news.

Lia decided not to worry about it. What was done was done.

"We won't be bothered here," Zach said. "It's too far out of the way for your typical paparazzi. They'll find easier quarry to harass." He stood with his hands in his pockets—he was wearing khakis and a muted aloha shirt—and looked gravely down at her. "How are you feeling? Do you need to rest?"

He was still hung up on the fact the doctor had said she needed more rest and less stress in her life. Everything had been fine with the baby, as she'd predicted. But the doctor had given him something new to worry about.

"I slept on the plane. I'm fine."

"Then you should eat," he said. "I'll go see what we have." He started to turn away, but she put a hand on his arm to stop him. Sparks sizzled into her nerve endings, as always, when she touched him.

She wanted to melt into him, like butter in a hot pan. He looked down at where her hand rested on his arm, and she remembered that she'd meant to say something. That it was odd and awkward if she did not.

"You work so hard to avoid me," she said. "It's not necessary."

That wasn't what she'd intended to say, but it was too late

to take the words back. They hung in the air between them, hovering like candle smoke.

His eyes were dark, fathomless, as he looked at her. Studied her like something he'd never encountered before. Her pulse skittered along merrily, and she forced herself to drop her hand away from the bare skin of his arm.

"You noticed," he said softly. "And here I thought I was so subtle."

Her head snapped up as pain sliced into her. Yes, she'd known he was avoiding her—but to hear him admit it dragged on the same nerve that had made her question her worth since she was a little girl. It should not hurt so much, but it always did.

She knew her worth was not determined by others, and yet she could never quite appease that lonely little girl inside who was still looking for acceptance.

"I noticed." She dropped her gaze, swallowing against the ridiculous lump in her throat, and his fingers came up to slide along her cheek. His touch made heat leap and tangle in her veins. If this heat were a light inside her, it would glow wherever he touched her.

"You pushed me away, *cara*. I was respecting your wish."

"I—I don't know what my wish is," she said truthfully. "I just know that you confuse me."

His gaze sharpened. "Why are you confused, Lia? I think you know what I want."

It took her a minute to answer. "I do," she finally said. "But I don't know why."

He blinked. And then he laughed. The sound burst from him, loud and rich and unexpected. Lia stared at him, her cheeks heating. A tiny thread of irritation began to dance through her. She crossed her arms and stared him down.

He stopped laughing at her, but he was still smiling. "Damn, I needed that." He put his hands on her upper arms.

where people had sex, sometimes even raunchy sex—but the idea she affected him that way, and that he had no problem saying it, both embarrassed and thrilled her.

"Allora," she said, resisting the urge to fan herself with both hands. "The things you say."

"Makes you hot, doesn't it?"

Lia put a hand over her eyes. *"Dio,"* she said.

Zach laughed and drew her hand away from her face. Then he took both her hands in his and held them in front of his body. "I like that you're still so innocent," he told her. "I like the idea of corrupting you."

A shiver washed over her as she imagined all the ways in which he might corrupt her. She'd had a taste of it, certainly, for two blissful days—but she knew there was more, knew they hadn't even scratched the surface of their need for each other.

"There's no time like the present," she replied, and then felt herself blushing harder than before if that were possible.

He led her through the gorgeous house with the soaring ceilings, the koa wood floors and overstuffed couches and huge open sliding doors, to a bedroom with a king-size bed and a breathtaking view of the ocean, with its white sand beaches, jagged black volcanic rocks and rolling surf.

The bed was on a platform, clothed in pristine white, and there was a television mounted on the opposite wall. She wondered who would ever want to watch television in a house like this, but then Zach stopped and tugged her into his arms again.

He kissed her softly, sweetly—too softly and sweetly to mean he was actually planning to make love to her, she realized, and then he stepped away.

"Take a bath, Lia. Have a nap. We'll have dinner on the lanai and watch the sunset. After that—" he shrugged "—anything goes."

* * *

Anything goes.

Lia couldn't get that thought out of her mind as she bathed and dressed. In spite of her insistence she'd slept on the plane, she had managed to fall into that giant king bed and drift off to sleep after she'd stared at the ocean for several minutes. It had surprised her to wake sometime later, when the sun was sliding down the bowl of the sky.

The doors to the outside were still open, and the ocean rolled rhythmically against the shore. A gentle trade wind blew through the room, bringing with it the scent of plumeria trees.

Now, Lia gazed at the ocean again as she stood in the open doors and gathered her courage before she went to meet Zach. Why, when she'd been ready earlier, did she suddenly feel as if a thousand hummingbirds were beating their wings in her belly?

Finally, she turned and strode from the bedroom, down the stairs and into the main living area. Zach wasn't on the lanai, and he wasn't in the living room. She continued to the kitchen, a huge room with koa wood cabinets and stainless-steel appliances. Zach was standing at the kitchen island, slicing fruit.

Lia blinked. It was such a domestic picture, and a surprising one. He looked up and smiled, and her body melted.

"You are fixing dinner?" she asked.

"It's nothing terribly exciting," he told her. "My repertoire is limited. But I can broil a fish, and I can make salad and cut up some fruit for dessert."

"You are a man of many talents," she said.

One eyebrow lifted. "I am indeed. I look forward to showing you some of those talents in detail."

Lia blushed and a grin spread over Zach's face. "You like embarrassing me," she said.

He walked over with a piece of pineapple and handed it to her. She popped it in her mouth, nearly moaning at the juicy sweetness.

"Not at all," he said as he went back over to the island. "I find it charming that you blush over such things."

"Charming," she repeated, as if it were a foreign word. Her family had never found her charming. They'd never thought she was anything but a nuisance. Except for Nonna, of course.

He picked up the platter. "Come out to the lanai and I'll bring everything," he told her.

"I can take the fruit."

He handed it to her and then went back for the salad. When they reached the table on the lanai—a table set with simple dishes and silverware—he set the salad down and took the fruit from her. Then he tugged her into his arms and kissed her.

"Yes, charming," he said. "I've never known anyone as innocent about such things as you are."

He let her go and pulled out her chair for her. As she sat, she looked up at him, her chest tightening at the emotions filling her. Emotions she really didn't want to spend much time analyzing. She already knew she cared too much. Did she need to know more than that?

"I don't like blushing like a nun in a locker room," she said. "It's ridiculous."

He laughed. "Like I said, charming."

He went and retrieved the rest of the food, and then they sat on the lanai with a view of the blue, blue ocean, and a big orange ball sinking into it. They ate fresh fish and talked about many things, none of them singularly important, but all important in the bigger picture of getting to know each other.

Lia learned that Zach liked to read biographies and military treatises, and that he'd defied his father by going to the

Air Force Academy rather than Harvard. She also learned that he managed his family's charitable foundation, and that he'd met Taylor Carmichael in his work supporting veterans' causes.

"Why did you drop the medal?" she asked, and then wanted to kick herself when he stiffened slightly.

But he took a sip of his wine and relaxed. "It's something the military does automatically, writing you up for medals when you've been in combat. But I didn't want it. I didn't want any of them."

Her heart pinched at the darkness in his tone. "But why?"

He kept his gaze on the ocean for a long time, and her pulse thrummed hot. She berated herself for pushing him, and yet she felt like she would never know him if she didn't ask these things. He was her husband, the father of her child, and she wanted to know who he was inside.

He turned to her, his dark eyes glittering hot. "Because six marines died saving me, Lia. Because I was drugged and I didn't do anything but lay there while they fought and died. They worked so damn hard to save me, and I couldn't help them. They died because of me."

Lia swallowed the lump that had formed in her throat. "I'm sorry, Zach," she said. She reached for his hand, squeezed it. She was encouraged when he didn't snatch it away. "But I think they died because they were doing their job, not because of you."

"You aren't the first to say that to me," he said, rubbing his thumb against her palm. "Yet I still have trouble believing it. I'm treated like a hero, and yet I haven't earned the right to be one. They were the heroes."

She hurt for him. He looked stoic, sitting there and staring out at the ocean beyond, and she wanted to wrap her arms around him and hold him tight. She fought herself, fought her natural inclination not to reach for him because of her fear of being rejected. In the end, the fear won.

"I doubt anyone thinks they weren't heroes," she said hotly, because she was angry with herself and angry with him, too. "They had jobs to do, and they did them. But they died because the enemy killed them. No other reason."

His expression was almost amused when he turned it on her. Except there was too much pain behind that gaze to ever be mistaken for amusement. "How fierce you are, *cara*. One wonders—do you have a limit? Would you, for instance, stop defending me if I crossed the line?"

CHAPTER TWELVE

SHE WAS LOOKING at him curiously, her brows drawing down over her lovely eyes. He could tell she was grappling with herself, with the things he was saying. Did she want to run? Did she want to lock herself in her room, away from him?

He almost wished she would. It would make things so much easier.

Because he was enjoying this too much, sitting here on the lanai with her and talking about their lives while they ate and watched the sun sink into the sea. He couldn't remember ever enjoying a woman's company the way he did hers. He loved women, loved sex, but companionship? He'd never thought of that before. Never cared. The old Zach changed women the way he changed clothes—frequently and as the situation dictated.

But, with Lia, he enjoyed the simple pleasures of spending time with her. It was a dangerous thing. Because she made him feel as if he could be normal again, when he knew he never could. He'd changed too much to ever go back to what he'd been before.

In the beginning, he'd thought it was possible. He'd thought the dreams would go away with time. That's what everyone said he needed: time. Time was the great healer. Time made everything better. Time, time, time.

He'd had time. More than a year's worth, and nothing was

the same. He had to accept that it never would be. He might always be plagued by dreams and fears, the same as he was plagued with unpredictable headaches. Those had changed his ability to fly forever, so why did he think time could fix the other stuff?

It couldn't. She couldn't.

"What line?" she asked, her voice soft and strong at once. As if she was challenging him. As if she didn't believe him. His chest felt tight as emotions filled him. This woman—this sweet, innocent woman—had faith in him. It was a stunning realization. And a sobering one.

He didn't want to fail her. And he didn't want to fail their child.

Another paradigm-shifting realization.

"It's nothing," he said, surprised at the trembling in his fingers as he reached for his wine. "Forget it."

She kept staring at him, her eyes large and liquid. "You are a man of integrity and honor," she said. "I do not doubt that at all."

"I tried to pay you off and send you away, Lia. Or have you forgotten?"

She picked up her glass. "I have not. But I understand why you did it."

"Because I'm an arrogant bastard with an unhealthy sense of self-importance?" He meant it to be self-deprecating, but he recognized the truth in it, too. He'd had his family consequence drummed into him from birth, after all.

"I wouldn't have put it that way," she said carefully, and he laughed.

She looked at him in confusion, and he didn't blame her. Just a moment ago, the conversation had been so serious, so dramatic. Now that it had moved away from the deeply intense and dark things residing in his soul, he could find humor in her reaction.

"Because you are too sweet," he said. He reached for her hand. The heat that sparked inside him was always surprising.

She frowned. "I don't feel particularly sweet. I feel quite cross at the moment, actually."

He brought her hand to her mouth, nibbled the skin over her knuckles. "I think I know how to change that," he murmured.

Lia's insides were melting. She didn't want to melt just yet, but she realized she had no choice in the matter. Sparks were zinging and pinging inside her like a fireworks display on New Year's eve.

She was still concerned about the things he'd said, about the self-loathing beneath his mask, but it seemed the subject was now closed. She'd been allowed a peek at the raw, tormented nature of Zach Scott, but now he was wrapped up tight again and she wasn't getting in.

She wanted to know the man who dreamed, who worked hard to make those speeches and ignore the triggers that could send him spiraling out of control. She wanted to touch the heart of him, she realized.

The way he'd touched hers.

He tugged her toward him until she got up and went to his side. Then he was pulling her down on his lap, tilting her back in his arms. His eyes gleamed with heat, and a hot wave of longing washed through her with the same kind of relentless surge of the ocean beyond.

"No more talking, Lia," he said, his fingers gliding over the skin beneath her collarbone.

When his lips replaced his fingers, her head fell back against the chair. His mouth moved over her, teasing, tormenting. The ocean pounded the shore a few yards away, and the trade winds blew, and Lia shuddered and gasped and knew she'd found heaven.

Her heart hurt with everything she felt: passion, hot and bright; fear, cold and insidious; and love, warm and glowing, like the sun as it had been right before it sank into the sea. There was a rightness about this, a rightness that felt like destiny and perfection.

She was meant to be here, and Zach was meant to be the man she shared her life with. She shivered again as he unbuttoned her shirt and peeled it back to reveal her shoulders and the soft swell of her breasts against the silk of her bra.

"Bellissimo," he said, his voice a silky purr. *"Ho bisogno di te, Lia."*

I need you.

Lia shivered again, her entire body on fire from tip to toes as his gaze raked her with that naked hunger she'd come to crave.

"Yes," she said. "Oh, yes."

His mouth came down on hers, and she was lost to anything but this molten hot fire between them. She wrapped her arms around him and shifted in his lap—and felt the hard evidence of his arousal pressing against her bottom.

His body tightened beneath her—and then all that beautiful power was lifting her, carrying her into the house while she clung to him and pressed kisses to his jaw, his neck, the delicious skin of his collarbone.

Soon, she was on her feet in the master suite. The doors were still slung open to let in the breezes, but they were completely alone out here on this remote stretch of beach. Zach stripped away her silky top and tailored trousers until she stood before him in nothing but her bra and a tiny scrap of silk that covered her sex.

His eyes darkened as they drifted over her, and a thrill shot through her.

"You look good enough to eat, Lia," he purred.

A fresh wave of heat pulsed inside her. She was wet, hot, and she wanted him.

But she couldn't move. She couldn't take those three steps to him, couldn't wrap her arms around him and be a wanton, seductive woman. Always she feared she wouldn't do it right, that he'd disapprove, or that he'd push her away and tell her she wasn't good enough, after all.

She knew better, she really did. But when you'd believed something your entire life, it was difficult to suddenly stop in a moment where every gesture, every touch, every look, set off firestorms inside. You'd do anything to keep the storm happening, anything to keep feeling the sweet heat. You would not take a risk.

He took a step toward her, his big body menacing—but in a good way. In a hard, protective, thoroughly delicious way.

"Do you want to touch me?" he asked.

She could only nod her head.

"Do it, then," he told her. "Touch me wherever you want. However you want."

"You have too many clothes on," she said, and blushed.

His laugh was deep, sexy, sinful. "Take them off, then."

She moved toward him, her fingers fumbling with the buttons of his shirt until she could finally push it free. It fell off his shoulders and landed in a pile at his feet. The shorts he'd changed into hung low on his body, revealing ridges of hard muscle and the perfect slash of hip bones.

She wanted to run her tongue along those bones. Wanted to dip it into the hollow of his abdomen, and then slide it down to the thick, hard length of his penis. But she didn't. She just stood and gaped like a kid in a candy store.

Zach swore, and then he was unbuttoning his shorts and shoving them down. His underwear went with them until he stood before her gloriously naked. His penis jutted out proudly, and his warrior's body made her mouth water.

She forgot herself. She reached for him.

But he reached for her, too, and soon they were lost in each other, kissing and touching and feeling what they'd missed for the past few weeks.

Lia wrapped herself around him until he put his hands on her bottom and lifted her. Her legs scissored around his waist as he carried her the few steps to the bed and tumbled her backward onto it.

"I wanted to seduce you slowly. But I can't wait, Lia," he managed finally, the hard ridge of his erection riding against the silk of her panties.

"Me, neither," she said—panted, really.

He rose up above her, jerked her panties down her legs and discarded them—and then he was back, pushing inside her until they were joined completely.

This, she thought, eyes closed, back arched, this utter perfection of his body so deeply within hers. This was what she wanted. What she needed.

His mouth fused to hers as he began to move. He wound his fingers into hers, pushed her arms above her head and proceeded to devastate her utterly with his lovemaking.

Days passed. Glorious sex- and sun-drenched days. They didn't talk about the military again, didn't talk about Zach's dreams. He slept with her at night, though she hadn't believed he would. The first night, when they'd made love and she was so thoroughly languid that she couldn't have moved if her life depended on it, he'd alarmed her by climbing from the bed and gathering his clothes.

When she'd asked him where he was going, he'd informed her he was going to his room. She'd sat up, the sheet tucked around her still-naked and glowing body, and wanted to cry. He'd told her it was best for them both, and that it wasn't her. It was him. She knew what he meant, but it still hurt to see him willing to walk away when she would have gladly walked across a room of broken glass just to be by his side.

He'd left her alone, and she'd turned to stare out at the ocean glowing beneath a full moon. The waves crashed against the shore, broke against the jagged rock cliffs that dotted the shoreline, and she felt as if her heart was broken and jagged, too.

Fifteen minutes later, Zach had returned. When he'd slipped into bed with her, she'd been unable to contain the small cry that erupted from her. He'd pulled her close, his mouth at her throat, and told her he wanted to try to stay with her.

She'd put her arms around him, threaded her fingers into that silky hair and nearly wept with relief and fierce joy.

They had not slept. Not at first. No, within minutes, Zach was inside her again, his body taking hers to heights that made the peak of Mount Everest look like an afternoon trek up a tiny foothill.

Finally, they crashed to the bottom again and fell asleep, entangled in each other's arms.

The days began to pass, each one as perfect and heart-breaking as the last. They spent hours making love, hours in the sunshine—floating in the pool, lying on the beach—and didn't leave the house to go anywhere. A service did the shopping and cleaning for them, so all they had to worry about was fixing their meals.

Zach did a great job at that, so there was nothing lacking in their self-imposed isolation. He'd been right, too, about the paparazzi. There were none on this lonely stretch of beach. They were opportunists, and opportunity was easier else-where.

The papers were filled at first with news of their hasty marriage and tropical honeymoon. Zach merely laughed and said it had all gone perfectly to plan. Eventually, though they were still news, they weren't on the front pages of the gossip rags anymore. Some Hollywood starlet and her latest drunk-driving conviction were taking center stage at the moment.

Lia spoke with her grandmother. The older woman seemed happy for her, though sad as well that she hadn't been at the wedding. Lia gave her some story about wildly beating hearts and true love being impatient, and her grandmother accepted it. Her cousin, apparently, was currently preoccupied with his own issues and wasn't inclined to worry about her fate at all.

She'd married a rich, influential man and that was good enough for the family. As for Rosa, Lia had been emailing back and forth with her sister quite frequently. They were both still wary, but there was a budding relationship that Lia thought might eventually grow into something she cherished.

Right now, however, she cherished Zach. She looked up from her book and let her gaze slide over him where he stood in the infinity pool, having just emerged from his swim. He was so very beautiful, hard and lean and fit in ways that made her mouth water.

And virile. She couldn't forget that one. The man did not tire out in the bedroom, or not until he'd exhausted himself pleasing her.

It was a good trait in a husband, she thought wickedly.

She was growing bolder in her experiments with his body. At first, she'd been afraid to try anything, afraid she would get it wrong and he'd not tell her because he didn't want to hurt her feelings.

But if she was getting it wrong, then he was a superb actor, because his gasps and groans and urgent touches and kisses spurred her to even greater experiments.

Like last night, when she'd taken him in her mouth as they sat out here on the lanai in the dark and listened to the ocean.

"Lia," he'd gasped as she'd freed him and then swirled her tongue around the head of his penis. And then he'd grabbed fistfuls of her hair and held her gently but firmly while she took him into her mouth. Her heart had beat so hard, so loud in her ears, but she could still hear him making those sounds of pleasure in his throat.

Before he'd orgasmed, however, he'd pulled her up and made her straddle him. She'd been wearing a silken nightie, no panties, and she'd sunk down on him while he held her hips and guided her.

She didn't remember much after that, except for the frantic way she'd ridden him until they'd both collapsed on the chaise longue. Much later, he'd carried her to bed and repeated the performance.

"What are you reading?" he said now, arraying his splendid form on the lounge beside her.

She held up her book. "I'm learning about the flowering plants of Hawaii. And how they make leis. Quite fascinating."

He groaned. "Please don't let me find you out pruning the plumeria one morning, searching for the perfect blooms."

Lia looked across at the single plumeria tree near the side of the house. It was tall, at least twenty feet, and filled with blooms whose perfume wafted over to her even now. "Don't be ridiculous," she said. "It's huge, and I'd need a ladder."

"You are definitely not getting on a ladder," he growled.

She laughed. "Of course not. I wouldn't dream of it."

His expression softened, his gaze raking over her. She got that warm glow inside that she always did. The words she'd not yet said to him welled behind her teeth, threatened to burst out into the open if she didn't work to contain them.

How could she tell him she loved him when that would be the ultimate soul-baring act she could perform? She'd be naked before him, naked in a way she could never take back. And he would have the ability to crush her. A single word. A single look.

He could crush her beneath his well-shod heel and she'd never recover.

Dio.

His brows drew down. "Are you feeling all right?" he asked. "Do you need to see a doctor?"

Lia rolled her eyes. It was a screen to cover all her raw, exposed feelings, but it was also a true reaction. He was incessantly worried about her health, which was sweet, but also managed to exasperate her.

"Zach, I'm fine. I have an appointment with the doctor on Oahu next week, remember?"

He continued to study her like she was a bug under a microscope. "Would you tell me if you were unwell? Or would you hide it?"

She blinked. "Why on earth would I hide such a thing?"

He looked at her for a long minute. And then he shrugged. "I have no idea. I just get the feeling that sometimes you aren't being completely honest about what you're feeling."

Her heart skipped a beat. Wow, he'd nailed it in one. But not for the reason he supposed. She reached out and grasped his hand. His skin was still cool from the pool. "I'm not used to sharing my life with anyone," she said truthfully. "I'm used to being self-reliant in many ways, but if I felt truly ill, I would tell you. I don't want anything to happen to this baby."

"Or you," he said, and her heart seemed to stop beating in her chest. A moment later, it lurched forward again, beating in triple time. She told herself not to read anything into that statement, but, oh, how her heart wanted to.

He turned away and reached for his tablet computer while her pulse surged and her heart throbbed. She wanted what he'd said to mean something. Wanted it desperately. But he sat there scrolling through his tablet so casually, and she knew that it hadn't meant a thing. Oh, he didn't want her to hurt herself, certainly.

But not because he didn't know what he'd do if she weren't here. Not because the air he breathed would suddenly grow stale without her. Not because his life would cease to be bright if she were not in it.

Lia turned away from him, her eyes pricking with tears, and picked up the virgin mai tai he'd fixed for her before he slipped into the pool. The trade winds blew so gently across her skin, and the sun was bright in the azure sky above. It was so perfect here, and she'd let herself be lulled by it.

But she had to remember there was nothing about this situation that was permanent. It could all end tomorrow, if he so chose. Lia shivered and tried not to imagine what would happen when it did.

In the end she didn't need to imagine a thing.

There was a storm in the middle of the night. It was a rare occurrence on Maui, because the trade winds and the air pressure didn't usually allow for it, but tonight there was thunder and jagged lightning sizzling over the ocean.

Lia woke with a jerk when a crack of thunder sounded close by. Zach was beside her, sitting up, his eyes wide.

"Zach?"

He didn't move. She reached for him. He jerked, then spun and pinned her to the bed. His eyes were wild, his skin damp. He growled something unintelligible.

"Zach, *caro*, it's me," she said. "It's Lia."

He was very still. "Lia?"

"Yes."

The tension in his body collapsed. He rolled away from her with a groan and lay on his back, an arm thrown over his eyes. "Jesus," he breathed. "I could have hurt you."

She propped herself on an elbow and leaned over him. "You wouldn't," she said, utterly convinced.

The arm fell away and his dark eyes gleamed at her as he drew in deep lungfuls of breath. "How can you be so sure? I'm a mess, Lia." He choked out something unintelligible. "A damn mess."

Fear was beginning to dance along the surface of her psyche. He frightened her, but not physically. "I don't believe that."

He laughed bitterly. "You're too damn trusting. Too naive. You have no idea what goes on in this world."

He threw the covers back and got out of bed while she sat there with her heart pinching and her chest aching. He yanked on a pair of shorts and stalked outside, onto the balcony, oblivious to the rain coming down.

Lia's first instinct was to stay where she was, to let him cool off. But she couldn't do it. She loved him too much, and she hated when he was hurting.

She climbed from the bed and put on her robe. Then she went to stand in the open door and look at him.

The rain washed over him, soaking his hair, running in rivulets down his chest. He looked lonely and angry and her heart went out to him. She knew what it was like to be lonely and angry. She wanted nothing more than to fix it for him.

"Zach, please talk to me."

He spun to look at her. "You don't want to hear what I have to say."

She took a step toward him.

He held a hand up to stop her. "Don't come out here. You'll get wet."

"It doesn't seem to be hurting you," she said, though she stopped anyway, folding her arms around her body. "And you're wrong. I do want to hear what you have to say."

He shoved his wet hair back from his face, but he didn't

make a move to come inside. Thunder rolled in the distance. A flash of lightning zipped along the sky, slicing it in two for a brief moment.

"I should have known better," he said. "I should have known it was a mistake to think this could work between us."

Her chest filled with chaotic emotion, tightening until she thought she wouldn't be able to breathe. But she held herself firmly, arms crossed beneath her breasts, and refused to let him see how much he hurt her. He thought she was naive, trusting. Unworthy.

It stung. But, worse, the idea she was a mistake threatened to make her fold in on herself.

"You can't mean that," she said tightly, though her brain gibbered at her to be quiet. To detach. To roll into a ball and protect herself. "These past couple of weeks have been perfect."

"Which is why it was a mistake," he snapped. "There's no such thing as perfect, not where I'm concerned."

"Because you don't deserve those medals?" she threw back at him, anger beginning to grow and spin inside her belly. "Because you have bad dreams and think you're so terrible?"

He took a step toward her, stopped. His hands clenched into fists at his side. He was close enough he could have reached out and touched her. But he didn't.

"You want to know the truth? I'll tell you," he grated. "The whole, sorry story."

He turned his back on her, walked over to the railing. The rain was lessening, but it was still coming down. When he turned back to her, his expression was tight.

"You've heard part of it. I broke my leg during the ejection. It hurt like hell, and I couldn't move much. But I'd landed near a protected ravine and hunkered down to wait.

I expected the enemy to find me first. But they didn't. The marines did. Only the enemy wasn't far behind."

Lia imagined him alone like that, imagined him waiting, and fear crawled up her throat, no matter that she'd heard him say this part before. She wanted to go to him, but she knew he didn't want her to. It made her desperate inside, but all she could do was listen.

"The medic drugged me," he said. "And I couldn't help them defend our position when they most needed me. Hell, I think I drifted in and out of consciousness. I have no idea how long it went on, but it seemed to take forever. They hit us with grenades, small-arms fire. It was ceaseless, and air support wasn't coming no matter how many times the marines called for it. One by one, the enemy picked off the marines, until it was one sergeant and me."

He didn't keep going, but she knew he wasn't finished. He turned away again, and she could see the tightness in his jaw, his shoulders. Zach was on edge in a way she'd only ever seen him when he was in the grips of a dream.

"Zach?"

He turned his head toward her. "Here's the part you don't know. The part no one knows. He gave me a pistol. Put it in my hand and removed the safety. And then he told me it was my choice when the enemy came. Shoot them, or shoot myself."

"No," she breathed as horror washed over her.

Zach's gaze didn't change, didn't soften. "Obviously," he said, "I didn't shoot myself. I didn't shoot anyone. Sometime in the night, the last marine died. And I wanted to shoot myself. I wanted it pretty badly."

"Oh, Zach…" Her eyes filled with tears.

"What you need to know, Lia, is that I tried to do it. I put the gun under my jaw." He put his finger just where he would have stuck the gun. Her heart lurched at the thought of him lying helplessly like that with so much death and destruction all around him. "But I couldn't pull the trigger."

The words hung in the air between them, like poison.

"I'm glad you didn't," Lia said fiercely, her throat a tight, achy mess. How close had he come? How close had she been to never, ever knowing him? It didn't bear thinking about.

"I can't forget that night. I can't forget how they all died, and how I could do nothing about it. I can't forget that I should have died with them."

Lia put a hand over her belly without conscious thought. "You weren't meant to die, Zach. You were meant to live. For me. For our baby."

His laugh was bitter, broken. "God, why would you think that? Why, after everything I just said to you, after the way I attacked you tonight, would you want me within a thousand miles of a child?"

She was starting to quake deep inside. Something was changing here. Something she couldn't stop. She was losing him. She'd begun to believe, over the past couple of weeks, that something was happening between them. Something good. She'd let herself be lulled by the sun and sea and the fabulous sex. Hadn't she had a glimmering of it earlier today by the pool?

"You didn't attack me. I startled you, but you have to remember that you let me go."

"What if I hadn't? You can't trust me, Lia. I can't trust myself."

"Then get some help!" she yelled at him. "Fight for me. For us."

He was looking at her, his chest rising and falling rapidly, and her hopes began to unfurl their wings. He could do this.

"It's not that easy," he said between clenched teeth. "Don't you think I've tried?"

"Then try again. For us."

He looked almost sad for a moment. "Why are you so stubborn, Lia? Why can't you just accept the truth? I told you I couldn't be a husband or a father. Now you know why."

Fear and fury whipped to a froth inside her. "Because I—" *I love you.*

But she couldn't say the words. They clogged her throat, like always, the fear of them almost more than she could bear. She'd worked hard not to love people who wouldn't love her back. She'd hidden inside her shell and shut everyone out.

Until Zach. Until he'd walked into her life and opened her up, exposing her soft underbelly. He'd made her love him. He'd made her vulnerable to this horrible, shattering pain again.

"Because what?" he said.

Lia swallowed the fear. She had to say the words. If she expected him to face his fear, then she had to face her own.

"Because I love you," she said, the words like razor blades. They weren't supposed to hurt. But they did.

Raw emotion flared in his eyes. And then his face went blank. He was shutting down, pulling up the cold, cool, untouchable man who lived inside him. She wanted to wail.

"That," he finally said, his voice so icy it made her shiver, "is a mistake."

"I don't believe that," she said on a hoarse whisper. "I refuse to believe that."

He came over to stand before her. She wanted to touch him, but she knew better than to try. Not now. Not when he was pushing her away. Not when her heart was breaking in two.

He put a finger under her chin and lifted until she had to look him in the eye. What she saw there eroded all her hopes.

"You're a good woman, Lia. You deserve better than this." His throat moved as he swallowed.

She feared what he would say, feared the look in his eyes. "Zach, no…"

He put his finger over her lips to silence her. "That's why I'm letting you go."

CHAPTER THIRTEEN

SICILY WAS JUST as Lia had left it, though she was not the same as she'd been when she'd left Sicily. She was bitterly angry. Hurt.

But one thing she was not, not ever again, was pitiful. She'd told her grandmother about the baby, because she couldn't hide it for much longer—and because she was no longer afraid of her family's reaction. Yes, it helped that she'd married the father. But she was still having this baby alone, regardless of what her family thought about that.

Far from being scandalized, Teresa had been thrilled to have a great-grandchild on the way. If the head of the family was upset about it, Lia didn't know it. Nor did she care.

Lia snipped lavender from the garden and dropped it into the basket sitting on the ground beside her. Then she wiped the back of her hand across her brow to remove the sweat before it could drip into her eyes. It was hot outside, crackling. Perhaps she should be inside, but she was going a little crazy just sitting there and reading books.

She was still in her cottage on her grandparents' estate, but she was in the process of purchasing an apartment of her own in Palermo. Once she'd returned to Sicily a month ago, she'd marched right into the family lawyer's office and told him she wanted her money. He'd blinked at her in a slow, lazy way that she feared meant he was about to deny her request or refer her to Alessandro, but instead he'd turned to his computer and began bringing up the family accounts.

She'd discovered that she had far more money than she'd thought. She would not need Zach's money to take care of their baby. It wasn't a fortune, but it would do.

It gave her great satisfaction to refuse a meeting with Zach's local attorney when he'd called to say he'd set up a bank account for her and needed her signature on some papers.

She would not take a dime of Scott money. Not ever.

The thought of Zach still had the power to make her feel as if someone had stabbed her with a hot dagger. She was so angry with him. So filled with rage and hate and—

No, not hate. Bitter disappointment. Hurt.

Her worst nightmare had come true when she'd given him her heart and he'd flung it back at her. He'd rejected her, just as she'd always been rejected by those to whom she wanted to mean something.

And it hadn't killed her. That was the part she'd found amazing, once she stopped crying and feeling sorry for herself.

She was hurt, yes, but she was here. Alive. And she had a life growing inside her, a tiny, wonderful life that she already loved so much. Her child would have everything she had not had. Friends, love, acceptance.

But not a father, she thought wistfully. Her baby would not have a father. Oh, Zach didn't want a divorce. He'd been very clear that she was still a Scott for as long as she wanted to be one, and that their child would have his name.

She'd met Zach's parents before she'd left. They'd been nice, if a bit formal, and they'd told her they wanted to be involved in their grandchild's life. So, her baby might not have a father, but he or she would have grandparents. She had agreed to return to the United States at least once a year, and they had indicated they would come to Sicily as often as she would allow it.

It had seemed far enough in the future that she figured she would have learned how to deal with her memories of Zach by then. She kept seeing him as he'd been that last night in Hawaii. Dark, tortured, dripping wet and so stubborn she wanted to put her hands around his throat and squeeze until he would listen to sense.

But there was no talking to Zach when he made up his mind. And, in his mind, he was a dangerous, damaged man who had no hope for the future. They'd boarded a jet the next morning after the storm on Maui. By nightfall they'd been back in D.C and then he'd disappeared.

Finally, on the fifth day, she'd decided she'd had enough. She'd made travel arrangements to Sicily and then she'd informed Raoul when she was leaving for the airport.

Zach had appeared very quickly after that. It had been an awkward meeting in which he'd told her he didn't want a divorce and that he would support her and their child. She'd sat through it silently, fuming and aching and wanting to throw things.

In the end, she'd left because it hurt too much to stay. Before she'd walked out the door the final time, she'd gone into his office and dropped the medal on his desk. He wasn't there, but she'd known he would see it. If it made him angry, so be it. It was the final tie she needed to cut if she was to move on with her life.

Apparently, her leaving hadn't fazed him in the least. It had been a month and she'd heard nothing from Zach, though she'd heard plenty from his local attorney. A man who was beginning to leave increasingly strident messages. Messages she had no intention of returning.

She clipped off some rosemary a little more viciously than necessary and dropped it in the basket. Then she got to her feet and put her hand in the small of her back. Her back ached quite a lot these days, but the doctor said everything was normal. She hadn't really started to show yet, though she'd had to get expansion bands for her pants and wear clothing that was loose around the middle. Soon, it would be time for maternity wear, but right now her maxi dress and sandals did just fine.

In the distance, the sea sparkled sapphire. It looked nothing like Maui, but it made her wistful nevertheless. She often found herself sitting on her little secluded terrazzo and gazing at the sea. She thought that if she did it enough, she would anesthetize herself to the pain.

So far, it hadn't worked. It was like reopening a wound each and every time.

She turned to make her way back to her cottage. The grounds sloped upward and the walk in this heat made her heart pound until she began to feel light-headed. She stopped for a moment, the basket slung over her arm, and wiped her forehead again. Her vision was growing spotty and her belly was churning. She groped in the basket for her water and came up with an empty bottle.

She could see her destination, see the terrazzo through the pencil pines and bougainvillea—and a man standing with his back to her. He had dark hair and wore a suit, and a swift current of anger shot through her veins, giving her the impetus she needed to keep putting one foot in front of the other.

She'd told Zach's lawyer that she didn't want to meet him. Yet he'd dared to come anyway, no doubt to try and force her to sign the documents that would make her the owner of a bank account with far too much money in it. She was not about to let Zach assuage his guilt that way. Let him choke on his millions for all she cared.

The man should not have made it through the estate's security, but he'd obviously sweet-talked his way inside. A red mist of rage clouded her vision as she trod up the lawn. Her stomach churned and her vision swam, but she was determined to make it. Determined to tell this man to take his briefcase full of papers and shove them where the sun didn't shine.

He might have sweet-talked Nonna into letting him onto the estate, but he wasn't sweet-talking her.

She stepped onto the tiles, her heart pounding with the effort. "How dare you," she began—but he turned around and the words got stuck in her mouth.

Her vision blurred and started to grow dark at the edges as bile rose in her throat. Too late, she recognized what was happening. Then everything ceased to exist.

Zach was miserable. He paced the halls of the local hospital where Lia had been taken. Her grandmother had promised to let him know what was happening, but she'd disappeared into the room with Lia and the doctor and hadn't come out again.

Zach shoved a hand through his hair and contemplated bursting through the door to Lia's room. This was not at all what he'd expected when he'd arrived today. He cursed himself for not being more cautious, for not calling her first. If he'd caused any harm to Lia or the baby, he would never forgive himself.

He stood with his fists clenched at his sides. He'd been such a fool, and now he couldn't shake the feeling he'd come too late.

That night, when he'd stood in the rain and told Lia about what had really happened—what had nearly happened— in that trench, he'd felt like the lowest kind of bastard. The kind who didn't deserve a sweet wife and a happy ending. He'd hated himself for turning on her during the storm— and earlier, in Palermo. He couldn't control the beast inside him, the slavering animal that reacted blindly, lashing out in fear and fury.

When he'd shoved her back on the bed, he'd known he couldn't take that risk ever again. He hadn't hurt her, as she'd pointed out, but he didn't trust that he was incapable of hurting her. He'd known then that he had to end it between them, and he had to do it immediately.

Letting her go had been the hardest thing he'd ever done. For days after she'd left, he'd walked around his house like a ghost, looking at the places she'd been, imagining her there within reach. Dying to touch her again and aching so hard because he couldn't.

He told himself he'd done the right thing. He was a beast, a monster, a man incapable of tenderness and love. He'd sacrificed himself for her safety, her happiness, and he'd felt honorable doing it.

But he'd also been miserable. And once he'd walked into his office and found the medal she'd left, he'd had a sudden visceral reaction that had left him on his knees, his gut hollow with pain, his throat raw with the howl that burst from him.

That's when he realized what he'd done. He'd sent her away, the greatest gift to come into his miserable life. In that moment, he knew what the hollowness, the despair, deep inside him was. He was in love with his wife. And he'd sent her away.

He'd wanted to go to her immediately, to beg her forgiveness—but he couldn't. He had to get himself straight first. He had to work on the things he'd shoved down deep. She'd told him to fight for her, and he'd been a coward.

Well, no more. He wasn't ready to quit. He wasn't going to quit. He'd done everything he could to come to her a changed man. Everything he could to deserve her.

He stared at the door to her room, ready to burst through

it and see if she was all right. It was taking too long and he was about to go crazy with fear. But then the door opened and the doctor came out.

"How is she?"

The man looked up from the chart he was holding. "Signora Scott will be fine. But she needs rest, *signore*. A woman in her condition should not be working outside in the heat of the day." He shook his head, then consulted the chart again. "She is dehydrated, but the fluids will take care of that. I want to keep her for observation, because of the baby, but she should be able to go home again in a few hours if all remains stable."

Shuddering relief coursed through him, leaving his knees weak. He put a hand on the wall to hold himself upright. He was about to ask if he could see her when Teresa Corretti came out of the room. She was an elfin woman, but she had a spine of steel. He'd seen that the instant he'd met her. Right now, she was looking at him with a combination of fury and concern.

"She will see you," she said. "But don't you dare upset her, young man. If you do, I will not be responsible."

He took her meaning quite well, especially since it was accompanied by a hard look that said she'd like to rip his balls off and feed them to him if he harmed a hair on her granddaughter's head.

She jerked her head toward the door. "Go, then. But remember what I said."

"Sì, signora," he replied. Then he took a deep breath and went inside.

His heart turned over at the sight of Lia in a hospital bed. She was sitting up, but her normally golden skin was pale, and her head was turned away from him as she gazed through the window at the parking lot beyond.

"Lia." His throat was tight. His chest ached. He'd been

through so much this past month, so many emotions. He hadn't thought seeing her again would be so hard, but he should have known better. He'd done his best to destroy her feelings for him, hadn't he?

"Why are you here, Zach?" she asked, still not looking at him.

He went over to the bed and sat in the chair beside it. He did not touch her, though he desperately wanted to. "To say I'm sorry."

Her head turned. Bright blue-green eyes speared into him. "You have come all this way to say you are sorry? For what? Breaking my heart? Abandoning your baby?" She waved a hand as if to dismiss him. "Take your apologies and leave. I do not need them."

His chest was so tight he thought he might start to hyperventilate at any moment. But he swallowed the fear and looked at her steadily. He could do this. He *would* do this.

"I'm ready to fight," he said.

She blinked. "Fight? I don't want to fight, Zach. Go away."

He took her hand this time. He had to touch her, needed to touch her. She flinched but did not try to pull away. Currents of heat swirled in the air between them, like always. It gave him hope.

"No, I want to fight for you. For us."

She turned her head away again, and his heart felt as if someone had put it in a vise and turned the screws. Her lip trembled, and something like hope began to kindle again inside his soul. If she was affected by his words, maybe it wasn't too late.

But it was a fragile hope. He'd done too much to her to deserve a second chance. He'd taken her love and thrown it away. He knew what kind of life she'd had, how she'd been deserted by her father and ignored by her family, and he'd pushed her away just the same as they had.

He'd discarded her when he should have fought for her. He'd figured it out finally. He just hoped it wasn't too late.

"You come here now and say this to me," she said, her voice thready. "Why should I believe you? What has changed in the past month? Do you dare to tell me you realized you cannot live without me?"

She'd turned back to him then, her voice gaining in intensity until he could feel the heat of her anger blistering through him. Her eyes flashed and her red hair curled and tumbled over her shoulders and he was suddenly unsure what to say. What if he got it wrong? What if she sent him away?

He couldn't let that happen. He'd do anything to prevent it.

"Yes," he said firmly. "That is exactly what I intend to say."

Lia's chest ached, and not from her fainting episode. She'd gotten overheated, her grandmother had told her. She'd fainted on her terrazzo, though Zach had caught her before she'd hit the hard marble. And then he'd carried her up to the house and ordered someone to call an ambulance.

Now she was here, feeling like a fool for getting too hot and fainting. She was also getting flustered by Zach's presence. By the words she could hardly believe he'd uttered.

They made her heart sing. But she was also afraid.

"I want you to come home," he said. "I want to be with you."

Lia swallowed. "I'm not sure I can do that," she said softly.

His expression was stark. Terrified.

"Leaving was hard," she continued, resolutely ignoring the ache in her heart, "but I've started to live my life without you. And if you drag me back, if you pull me into your life and then decide you can't handle a wife and child, I'm not sure I will survive that heartbreak a second time."

"I went to see a doctor," he told her quietly. His hand was

still wrapped around hers, and she felt the tremor shake him as he said those words.

"Oh, Zach." There was a lump in her throat.

"I can't guarantee I won't have dreams. I'm pretty sure I will have them. But I know how to deal with them now."

He stood, moved until he was so close she could reach up and touch him if she wanted to.

He pressed her hand to his heart. It beat hard and fast beneath her palm.

"I told the doctor about the gun and how I couldn't pull the trigger. And I'm taking medicine, Lia. It helps with the fear and anger. I didn't want to take it before. I thought I could handle it myself. But the truth is I can't. No one can. We aren't meant to handle these things alone."

Her vision blurred again, but this time it was due to the moisture in her eyes. "I'm glad you got help, Zach. Really glad." She turned her hand in his and squeezed. "But I'm still not sure coming back is the right thing. You hurt me when you sent me away, and I can't be hurt like that again. I can't let our baby be hurt, either."

He looked suddenly uncertain, as if he'd come across a roadblock he hadn't expected.

"And if I said I love you?"

Her heart went into free fall before soaring again. She told herself to be realistic, practical. To not simply accept what he said at face value because she'd wanted it for so long. She'd been disappointed so many times by her need to be loved. She would not let it rule her now.

"Why do you love me, Zach? Why now?"

He sank onto the chair beside the bed again. His eyes were intense, burning, as they caught hers and held.

"I love you because you give me hope. Because you see the good in me instead of the bad. Because you believe in me. Because you made me believe in myself." He sucked in a breath, his nostrils flaring. His voice, when he spoke again, was fierce. "I'm glad I lived, Lia. I'm glad I'm here with you, and even if you send me away, even if you never let me back in your life again, I won't regret a single moment I spent with you."

She felt a tear spill free and slide down her cheek. She dashed her hand over her face, as if she could hide her tears from him.

But he saw them, of course.

"It kills me when you cry," he said softly. "And it kills me to think I caused it."

Her heart squeezed. "I'm not crying because I'm unhappy. I'm hormonal."

It wasn't the truth, of course, but she stubbornly didn't want to admit she was crying because of him. She'd cried too much over him this past month already.

"I love you, Lia. I don't want you to cry. I want to make you happy. Always."

She was trembling hard now, but she turned away from him and tried to focus on the cars moving in the parking lot outside. How could she cross this bridge again? How could she make herself vulnerable once more to all the vicissitudes of a relationship with this man?

"I—I want to believe you. But I'm not sure I can."

"You can," he said. "I know you can. Isn't that what you said to me?"

She dropped her chin to her chest and sucked in a huge breath. She had said that to him. She'd said it and she'd been angry when he hadn't listened. When he'd denied it and sent her away.

How could she do the same thing to him? How could she be a coward, when he ultimately had not? He was facing his fears, finally. How could she be any different?

"I will try," she said softly. "That's the best I can do."

* * *

She left the hospital that evening. She'd thought she was going back to her grandmother's house, but when Zach turned a different direction, she could only look at him. He glanced over at her.

"I'm taking you to our home," he said. "It will be more private for us."

She lifted an eyebrow. "I wasn't aware we had a home in Sicily."

He shrugged. "Actually, it's a rental. If you like it, I'll buy it for you. And if you don't, I'll buy you another one somewhere else."

A little thrill went through her, in spite of her resolve to take this slowly and carefully. She'd agreed to try to believe he loved her, and that this could work between them, but she hadn't actually thought about what that would entail. Of course they would go to a home they shared. And of course they would be alone together.

So much for her resolve when her pulse picked up at the thought.

Zach took her to a large, beautiful villa with a view of the sea. She could tell because the lights of homes carpeting the island below them gave way to a vast inky darkness. The lights of a ship moved alone on that black surface, isolated from civilization.

She stood on the balcony and let the sea breeze ruffle her hair, feeling like that ship, adrift on an immense sea of uncertainty and fear.

"You should be sitting," Zach told her. "You've had a rough day."

"In more ways than one," she replied.

"Yes."

She felt bad for saying it then, for making him quietly accept her lingering animosity. But it was the only thing standing between her and complete capitulation, so she nursed it in wounded silence. Until it burst from her, like now.

"I'm sorry," she said, turning to him. He stood so near, hands in pockets, dark eyes trained on her.

"Don't be. I deserve it."

She sighed. "No. I'm just afraid, Zach. Afraid it won't be real."

"Maui," he said, his voice so quiet, and her heart pinched because he knew.

"Yes, Maui." She took a deep breath. "We had such a perfect time there. I thought there was something between us, and then it stormed and you became a stranger to me. You showed me that I didn't matter, that nothing we'd shared mattered."

"I'm more sorry for that than you know. But I was damaged, Lia, and I was afraid of that damage somehow spilling over onto you. You, the sweetest, most innocent woman I've ever known. How could I tarnish that brightness of yours with my darkness?"

"You can't be undamaged now," she said, shaking her head. "Not in a month. Not ever. So how do you propose to reconcile what you think of as damage—which I think of as life, by the way—with our relationship now? Will the first dream or episode send you running again?"

He sighed. "I deserve every bit of your condemnation. No, I am not undamaged. But none of us are, are we? I'm learning to cope with that." He paused for a moment. "I found the medal you left behind. I put it with the others. And they're in my desk drawer at home, where I see them every day when I open it. I earned them with my blood and sweat and tears. And I owe it to those who gave their lives for me to honor their memories by not running from my own."

A chill slid down her spine as he spoke. And she knew, deep in her heart, that what he said was true. That he'd turned a corner somewhere in his journey and he was finally on the way to healing.

She took a step toward him, reached up and caressed the smooth skin of his jaw. "Zach," she said, her heart full.

He turned his face into her palm and kissed it. "I love you, Lia Corretti Scott. Now and forever. You saved me."

A dam burst inside her then. She went into his arms with a tiny cry, wrapped herself around him while he held her tight. This was what it meant to love and be loved. To belong.

"No, I think we saved each other."

"Does this mean you still love me?" he asked, his voice warm and breathless in her ear.

She leaned back so she could see his face. His beautiful, beloved face. "I never stopped, *amore mio*. I never could."

"Grazie a Dio," he said. And then he kissed her as a full moon began to rise from the sea, lighting their world with a soft, warm glow.

EPILOGUE

LIA WOKE IN the middle of the night. She sat up with a start, certain she'd heard a cry. It was raining outside, a typical summer storm. A jagged bolt of lightning shot across the sky, followed by a crack of thunder.

The bed beside her was empty, the sheets tossed back. She grappled on the nightstand for the baby monitor, but it was gone. Sighing, she climbed from bed and put on her robe. Then she padded out the door and down the hallway to the nursery.

Zach looked up as she entered. He was sitting in the rocking chair, cradling their son in his arms while the baby cooed and yawned. Zach smiled, and her heart lurched with all the love she felt for the two men in her life.

"I believe it was my turn," she said tiredly.

"I was awake," he said, shrugging.

"A dream?" she asked, thinking of the storm and worrying for him.

"I was dreaming, yes," he said. "But not about the war."

"You weren't?"

He looked down at their baby, his sexy mouth curling in a smile. "No. I dreamed I was flying. And then I dreamed I was on a beach with you."

"What happened then?"

"I could tell you," he said, slanting a look up at her. "But I'd far rather show you."

Heat prickled her skin, flooded her core. "I'll look forward to it," she said softly.

"Give me a few minutes." His gaze was on his son again.

Lia pulled a chair next to the rocker and sat down beside him. Zach reached out and took her hand in his, and they sat there with their baby until his little eyes drifted shut. Gently, Zach placed him in his crib—and then he took Lia by the hand and led her back to their bedroom.

Later, as she lay in his arms and drifted off to sleep, she knew she'd gotten everything she ever wanted.

Love. Family. Belonging.

* * * * *

*Read on for an exclusive
interview with Lynn Raye Harris!*

BEHIND THE SCENES OF
SICILY'S CORRETTI DYNASTY

It's such a huge world to create—an entire Sicilian dynasty. Did you discuss parts of it with the other writers?

Oh, yes! We started an email loop and discussed where to set the Corretti estates and whether the wedding, which kicks off the whole thing, would be in a chapel or a cathedral, etc. We also discussed character interactions and how they felt about their histories.

How does being part of the continuity differ from when you are writing your own stories?

Well, one of the hardest parts of writing a continuity is finding connection with the characters. When they are your own creation it's much easier to find that connection than when you are given a brief about them. But it eventually happens, and then you have fun!

What was the biggest challenge? And what did you most enjoy about it?

This time, for me, the biggest challenge was writing an American hero. That's probably an odd thing to say, since I am an American, but I found Zach far more difficult because of it. Add in his military service, and I really had a difficult time. Not because I don't know anything about the military—but because I know too much! My husband was in the air force, though he didn't fly planes, and I'm pretty familiar with military life. It was a challenge to balance that element in the story, probably because I was too concerned with making it correct.

As you wrote your hero and heroine was there anything about them that surprised you?

Zach told me something that surprised me. He tells Lia, too, so you'll get to see what it is. It's a very dark thing, and we both ached for him that he's been living with this guilt and self-loathing.

What was your favorite part of creating the world of Sicily's most famous dynasty?

The research! Who doesn't like looking at pictures of Sicily and reading about the culture? Regrettably, my characters don't spend a lot of time there, but it was still fun!

If you could have given your heroine one piece of advice before the opening pages of the book, what would it be?

Chin up, babe.

What was your hero's biggest secret?

I can't tell! It's in the book.

What does your hero love most about your heroine?

Her sweetness and strength. She believes in him and that means a lot.

What does your heroine love most about your hero?

He's honorable and he cares a great deal about doing the right thing.

Which of the Correttis would you most like to meet and why?

Oddly enough, I think I'd like to meet Teresa Corretti! She's the matriarch who kept the whole thing together when it should have failed long before. She's a strong woman used to dealing with lots of arrogant men. I imagine she's the strength behind the family throne, really, though they don't quite know it.

Mills & Boon® Hardback
October 2013

ROMANCE

MEDICAL

0913 GEN STD HB

Mills & Boon® Large Print
October 2013

ROMANCE

The Sheikh's Prize	Lynne Graham
Forgiven but not Forgotten?	Abby Green
His Final Bargain	Melanie Milburne
A Throne for the Taking	Kate Walker
Diamond in the Desert	Susan Stephens
A Greek Escape	Elizabeth Power
Princess in the Iron Mask	Victoria Parker
The Man Behind the Pinstripes	Melissa McClone
Falling for the Rebel Falcon	Lucy Gordon
Too Close for Comfort	Heidi Rice
The First Crush Is the Deepest	Nina Harrington

HISTORICAL

Reforming the Viscount	Annie Burrows
A Reputation for Notoriety	Diane Gaston
The Substitute Countess	Lyn Stone
The Sword Dancer	Jeannie Lin
His Lady of Castlemora	Joanna Fulford

MEDICAL

NYC Angels: Unmasking Dr Serious	Laura Iding
NYC Angels: The Wallflower's Secret	Susan Carlisle
Cinderella of Harley Street	Anne Fraser
You, Me and a Family	Sue MacKay
Their Most Forbidden Fling	Melanie Milburne
The Last Doctor She Should Ever Date	Louisa George

Mills & Boon® Hardback
November 2013

ROMANCE

Million Dollar Christmas Proposal	Lucy Monroe
A Dangerous Solace	Lucy Ellis
The Consequences of That Night	Jennie Lucas
Secrets of a Powerful Man	Chantelle Shaw
Never Gamble with a Caffarelli	Melanie Milburne
Visconti's Forgotten Heir	Elizabeth Power
A Touch of Temptation	Tara Pammi
A Scandal in the Headlines	Caitlin Crews
What the Bride Didn't Know	Kelly Hunter
Mistletoe Not Required	Anne Oliver
Proposal at the Lazy S Ranch	Patricia Thayer
A Little Bit of Holiday Magic	Melissa McClone
A Cadence Creek Christmas	Donna Alward
Marry Me under the Mistletoe	Rebecca Winters
His Until Midnight	Nikki Logan
The One She Was Warned About	Shoma Narayanan
Her Firefighter Under the Mistletoe	Scarlet Wilson
Christmas Eve Delivery	Connie Cox

MEDICAL

Gold Coast Angels: Bundle of Trouble	Fiona Lowe
Gold Coast Angels: How to Resist Temptation	Amy Andrews
Snowbound with Dr Delectable	Susan Carlisle
Her Real Family Christmas	Kate Hardy

Mills & Boon® Large Print
November 2013

ROMANCE

His Most Exquisite Conquest	Emma Darcy
One Night Heir	Lucy Monroe
His Brand of Passion	Kate Hewitt
The Return of Her Past	Lindsay Armstrong
The Couple who Fooled the World	Maisey Yates
Proof of Their Sin	Dani Collins
In Petrakis's Power	Maggie Cox
A Cowboy To Come Home To	Donna Alward
How to Melt a Frozen Heart	Cara Colter
The Cattleman's Ready-Made Family	Michelle Douglas
What the Paparazzi Didn't See	Nicola Marsh

HISTORICAL

Mistress to the Marquis	Margaret McPhee
A Lady Risks All	Bronwyn Scott
Her Highland Protector	Ann Lethbridge
Lady Isobel's Champion	Carol Townend
No Role for a Gentleman	Gail Whitiker

MEDICAL

NYC Angels: Flirting with Danger	Tina Beckett
NYC Angels: Tempting Nurse Scarlet	Wendy S. Marcus
One Life Changing Moment	Lucy Clark
P.S. You're a Daddy!	Dianne Drake
Return of the Rebel Doctor	Joanna Neil
One Baby Step at a Time	Meredith Webber